WE KNOW YOUR SECRET

SEBASTIAN GREGORY

POCKETBOOK PRESS

First Edition: September 2025

Published by Pocketbook Press
Las Vegas, Nevada

ISBN: 978-1-234567-89-0

Printed in the United States of America

Cover art by Cici Teegan

To fans of 80s and 90s horror. This one is for you.
I hope you enjoy reading this as much as I enjoyed
writing it.

Acknowledgements

Writing *We Know Your Secret* has been a wild roller-coaster of nostalgia, late-night writing sprees, and endless "just one more edit" promises that turned into entire weekend sessions.

First, to Tracey and Marie, my brilliant creative partners. I couldn't have done this without you. Thank you for the brainstorming sessions, the constant encouragement, and for indulging my random texts at all hours without judgment. Your storytelling instincts and editorial insight kept me grounded, and your willingness to share in my deep love for all things 90s made the process that much more fun.

To my husband, Mike, and our children, Noa and Logan. Thank you for your endless patience, humor, and understanding when I disappeared into fictional worlds and became irritable when interrupted. You remind me every day what matters most.

To Melanie, for reading my draft and lifting me up when I doubted myself.

To Dan, for making me feel smarter and better than I am.

To Rehn and Mariette, for our group texts, goal setting, and unwavering encouragement.

To my parents and siblings, for your love, support, and for giving me a childhood bursting with memories (and plenty of material) to fuel my stories. Thanks for surviving the 90s with me.

To my pets Duchess, Princess Crystal, Baby Blue, and Freeway. Thank you for your quiet companionship during long writing sessions and for reminding me to pause, breathe, and step away when I needed it most. Your antics brought laughter, your loyalty brought peace, and somehow I focused better with you curled up beside me.

Finally, to my Pocketbook Press family. Thank you for believing in me and the retro stories I want to tell.

PROLOGUE

The living room's only light came from a corner lamp casting a soft, intimate glow over the couple on the couch. The cordless phone on the counter buzzed. *8:07 PM* flashed across its dim display.

The TV hummed in the background, a late-night rerun of *America's Most Wanted* flickering across the screen. The program cut to a commercial break and a Mentos ad played, the jingle cheerful and out of place. Then came the Taco Bell chihuahua, barking about two tacos for 99 cents, followed by a teaser for the third season premiere of *Friends*

The couple didn't even glance at the screen, too tangled in each other to notice the man standing in the doorway, still as death, watching with eyes that didn't blink.

The man's wife, Laura, petite, sharp-featured, her long auburn hair loose and unbothered, just like her, leaned into another man's chest. *His* couch. *His* wife. She laughed at something he'd said. The sound was light, effortless. Free.

A laugh he hadn't heard in years.

For a moment, the man stood frozen, his fists clenched so tightly his nails bit into his palms. The Sony Discman clipped to his belt pressed against his hip, the headphones dangling uselessly around his neck. He'd gone for a late-night walk to clear his head, Depeche Mode's *Songs of Faith and Devotion* his chosen sound-track. But now, as he stood there, the music felt like a cruel joke.

"Eric," Laura shouted his name in surprise, standing up. Her voice was sharp, jolting him from his daze. "What are you doing here?"

The man beside her on the couch—*Matt*, Eric vaguely recalled, a coworker of Laura's—stood up, his expression a mixture of guilt and defiance.

"Look, man," Matt started, raising his hands in a placating gesture, "we don't want any trouble."

Eric's laugh was bitter. "Oh, really? Then maybe don't screw my wife in my fucking house."

"Eric, stop," Laura said, stepping between them. "You're drunk. You don't live here anymore. You know that."

The words stung, not because they weren't true but because of how dismissive they sounded. As if he was nothing more than an inconvenience to her.

He *had* stopped at the liquor store on his walk and downed half a bottle of Old Crow before deciding to visit the house. And he *didn't* live there anymore. She had made him move out months ago.

"You think I'm just gonna walk away?" he spat, his voice rising. "While you do...this?" He gestured wildly at the couch, the empty wine glasses, the crumpled edges of Chinese takeout on the coffee table. "In the home we built? In the home where we raised our child?"

Laura's face hardened at the mention of their daughter. "I'm sorry. I didn't want it to happen this way, but we're over, Eric. You know that. You've known that for a long time."

Something inside him snapped. The hurt, the betrayal, the months of her cold indifference all coalesced into a single, blinding moment of rage.

Matt moved first, stepping toward Eric as if to reason with him, but Eric was faster. His hand shot out, grabbing the heavy glass ashtray from the end table. The motion was almost reflexive, as if his body had acted before his mind could process it.

The ashtray hit Matt's temple with a sickening crunch. Matt crumpled to the floor, his eyes wide and unfocused. Laura screamed, the sound piercing and raw, but Eric barely heard it over the pounding in his ears.

"You bastard!" Laura lunged at him, her nails raking across his face. Eric stumbled back, blood trickling from the fresh scratches, but the adrenaline coursing through him dulled the pain.

He grabbed her wrists, twisting them until she cried out. "You did this," he growled, his face inches from hers. "You *made* me do this."

She stared at him, her defiance giving way to fear. For a brief moment, he hesitated. This was Laura, the woman he'd loved, the mother of the child they had just sent off to college. But then he glanced down at Matt's lifeless body, the blood oozing from his head, the betrayal that seeped into every corner of the room like a toxic cloud.

There was no going back.

In a blur of motion, he shoved Laura backward. Her head struck the edge of the coffee table with a dull thud, and she collapsed beside Matt, her body unnervingly still. A slow, dark pool of blood seeped from the back of her skull, spreading across the hardwood floor.

Eric stood there, panting, his vision swimming, the room tilting around him. For a moment, he just stared at her. Then he dropped to his knees beside her, pressing his fingers to her neck. Searching for a pulse.

Nothing.

He yanked his hand away, his chest heaving.

The flickering TV screen caught his eye. *America's Most Wanted* droned on, John Walsh's grim face filling the screen as he recounted the details of yet another violent crime, just like he did every week.

The irony wasn't lost on Eric.

The next hour passed in a blur. In the garage, he yanked a rolled-up tarp from the wall and dragged it back inside. He spread it across the floor, then wrestled Laura's body onto it. The plastic crackled as he folded it over her, sealing her away. Then came Matt—heavier, harder to maneuver, his limbs refusing to bend the way he needed. Grunting, he forced the tarp around him, cinching it tight before dragging the two bundles across the floor. His arms trembled, sweat stinging his eyes, but he managed to heave them, one after the other, into the trunk of Laura's car. When the lid finally slammed shut, he staggered back, hands braced on his knees, head spinning.

Then it was back to the living room, where he moved on autopilot, scrubbing at the blood with an old towel, his hands trembling as he worked the deep red stain out of the hardwood. It smeared at first, soaking into the grain, but he didn't stop. He doused the spot with bleach, his nostrils stinging from the fumes, his heartbeat thudding in his ears.

The broken wine glasses went into a thick trash bag along with the ruined ashtray, wrapped in the towel so the shards wouldn't tear through the plastic. He gathered anything that might leave a trace, wiped down the coffee table, checked for stray droplets on the rug, even scrubbed under his nails.

When he finished, he stood in the center of the room, chest heaving, sweat clinging to his skin. The room was still, except for the ticking clock. He hadn't realized how long it had taken.

The house looked the same as the day he'd left it. The mantle still held the framed wedding photo, coated in a fine layer of dust, as if forgotten rather than discarded.

Had she simply overlooked it, or had she chosen to leave it there?

A stack of VHS tapes lined the shelf, their edges frayed from use. He ran a finger along the spines, remembering moments on the couch watching *Saturday Morning Cartoons* with his daughter Ellie while Laura made breakfast in the kitchen. He could still feel the warmth of his daughter curled against him and hear the way she'd laugh at the same jokes no matter how many times she'd seen them.

For a fleeting moment, something stirred in his chest. Maybe Laura hadn't erased him completely. Maybe she had made a mistake. Maybe he had reacted too harshly. Hadn't given her a chance to explain.

As he grabbed a trash bag from the kitchen, he noticed the refrigerator magnets they had bought on family vacations still clung to the door, pinning up faded takeout menus. And then there was Ellie's drawing, a crayon-scrawled family portrait she had made in fourth grade, still held up on the fridge after a decade. The colors had faded, the paper curled at the edges, but they had never taken it down.

His throat tightened. What had he done?

But it was too late for that now. He finished cleaning, eliminating every trace of what had taken place.

He told himself it was over. That he could move on once he disposed of the bodies. But how? What would he tell Ellie? He'd have to figure that out eventually.

For now, he had work to do.

Eric grabbed the keys to Laura's car, took one last glance at the house, at the life that was no longer his, and stepped into the garage. He scanned the cluttered shelves, then pulled down a shovel, its metal blade nicked and rusted. A pickaxe leaned in the corner; he dragged that out too. From a workbench drawer he yanked a pair of gloves and a flashlight, tossing them onto the passenger seat. One last look, one last breath, and he slid behind the wheel.

He was already feeling tired, but he knew the night was far from over. What he didn't know was just how long it would stretch and how much worse it would get.

CHAPTER 1

Lisa Turner hated chemistry. Not because she was bad at it—she wasn't—but because Mr. Donner had a way of making her feel like every mistake was personal.

Her dark hair was pulled back into a loose ponytail, and she wore a pale blue cardigan over a floral dress, her wire-rimmed glasses sliding down her nose. She looked more like a shy librarian than a junior in high school.

She stood at the lab station near the window, sleeves rolled up, goggles pressing awkwardly against her cheeks. Her partner, Ben Nguyen, quietly adjusted the Bunsen burner while Lisa reread their titration instructions for the third time.

The first attempt had gone wrong. Too much base. The second, not enough. Now they were on their third try.

Mr. Donner moved between stations, offering tips and quiet corrections. His shirt sleeves were rolled to the elbow, forearms flexing as he adjusted glassware. He spoke calmly, never raised his voice. But when he gave feedback, it always felt personal.

Lisa dipped the burette and started to release the solution into the flask. She could feel heat in her face and struggled to keep her hands from shaking. She glanced at the worksheet, still blank in the data section. Ben was writing their names in the corner.

She shouldn't have cared what Mr. Donner thought. She shouldn't have been watching him as he leaned over Alexis's lab bench.

But she did.

"Miss Turner," he said, suddenly beside her.

Lisa jumped, almost spilling the contents of the beaker.

"You're releasing too fast," he said. "Control the flow. Chemistry is patience, not instinct."

"Right," she muttered, adjusting the valve. "Sorry."

Mr. Donner stepped closer, gently taking the pipette to show her. His hands were steady, precise. His voice low. "Try again. Slowly."

Lisa nodded, barely breathing.

He moved on to the next station. Ben didn't look up from the worksheet.

"Dude's got radar for when we're screwing up," he muttered.

Lisa forced a small smile. "Yeah."

She tried again. Slower. But the color in the flask shifted too quickly. Another failed trial.

The bell rang. Mr. Donner clapped once. "Lab reports due Monday. I expect clean data."

Students groaned in frustration, gathering their things. Lisa didn't move.

Mr. Donner approached her. "Miss Turner," he said. Lisa looked up. "You'll need to repeat the experiment. Your titration endpoint was inconsistent in all three trials."

Lisa opened her mouth to protest, but decided not to. "Okay," she said instead.

His expression softened just slightly. "You're capable. Just slow down."

Then he walked away.

Lisa stayed where she was, staring at the flask. Ben had already left.

Redo it? Again?

She packed her things slowly, her hands tingling with frustration. She hated that she wanted his approval so badly. She hated that her first thought when he said her name wasn't embarrassment. It was a spark of something she didn't quite understand.

As she stepped into the hallway, students rushed around her. She forced herself to breathe deeply, pushing down the twist in her stomach. She caught a glimpse of her reflection in the trophy case glass. Cheeks flushed. Eyes too wide.

"Get a grip," she whispered to herself.

Then she adjusted her bag and walked toward her locker, where Katie, her best friend, was already waiting.

CHAPTER 2

Katie Lewis leaned against her locker, absent-mindedly turning the combination lock while her eyes drifted over the lively chaos of Ridgewood High. The familiar sounds of slamming locker doors and bursts of laughter echoed through the corridor.

A loud cluster of high schoolers passed by, backpacks slung low, voices sharp with laughter. Someone down the hall blasted *"California Love"* from a portable stereo, earning a sharp glare from Mrs. Haggerty, the math teacher, whose perm seemed to vibrate with disapproval.

Katie exhaled dramatically and stretched, her plaid flannel shirt riding up slightly over her faded Levi's.

Her blonde hair, now dyed purple, fell in loose waves around her face, radiating the kind of confidence only a seventeen-year-old with no regard for the future could pull off. She had a presence that made her a magnet for attention, whether she wanted it or not.

Across the hall, Katie's boyfriend, Tyler Jacobs, was tossing a Nerf football with one of his friends. He was the quintessential high school golden boy—blonde hair, blue eyes, athletic build. His varsity jacket hung casually over one shoulder, and he flashed the trademark smile that had gotten him out of more than a few detentions. He winked at Katie, who rolled her eyes but couldn't stop a smile from tugging at her lips.

They'd been together since the spring before junior year, right after Katie got dumped by a senior with a motorcycle and a "philosophy phase." Tyler had been steady, sweet, and calm. At first it was a rebound. Now, it was something more complicated. Comfortable. Real.

Maybe too real.

"Katie! Tyler's staring again," Lisa said, approaching with a stack of textbooks teetering in her arms.

Katie smirked, popping a piece of Bubble Tape into her mouth and holding the roll out to Lisa. "He can't help it. I'm irresistible."

Lisa cut a piece. "Thanks." She popped the gum into her mouth. "The only thing you're irresistible to is bad decisions and guys who peaked in middle school."

"That's way harsh. What's with you?"

"Ugh, I'm sorry. Chem lab sucked today," she said, shifting the books awkwardly to one arm. "Mr. Donner made me and Ben redo the titration experiment like three times. Even Ben looked ready to throw the beaker at the wall, and he's usually too nice to complain." Lisa sighed, clearly still stewing. "And of course Mr. Donner was hovering the whole time, watching me like I was about to blow something up."

Katie smirked. "Are you sure that's the reason he was watching you?"

Lisa hesitated, then muttered, "Shut up! He's just really...intense."

Katie smirked. "Sounds like your first lover's spat."

"Stop," Lisa shot back, her cheeks flushing as she nudged Katie with her elbow. "It's not like that."

"Uh-huh," Katie teased, grinning. "You know, for someone who says she doesn't care, you sure go red every time his name comes up."

Lisa groaned, letting her head fall back dramatically. "He's just—ugh, forget it. Let's go before you start turning this into some terrible porn scenario."

Katie laughed, slinging her bag over her shoulder. "Fine, but I'm keeping my eye on you. *Donner does Lisa* has a nice ring to it."

"Seriously, shut up," Lisa said again, but this time there was a reluctant smile tugging at her lips.

"Next time, just ditch like I did," Katie said, blowing a bubble and letting it pop audibly.

"Not everyone can charm their way out of class," Lisa said, glancing down at Katie's scuffed Converse sneakers. "Or get away with wearing those heinous shoes to school."

Katie shrugged, adjusting her flannel. "It's not charm, it's strategy. It's easy with the male teachers. You should try it sometime. And these shoes are very comfortable."

She tilted her head toward Lisa's books. "It's the weekend and we have plans. Leave some of that shit in your locker."

Lisa hesitated but relented, cramming half the books into her locker. "Fine, but if I forget any homework, it's your fault." She snapped the locker shut and turned back to Katie, who had already slung her denim backpack over one shoulder.

As Lisa let out a sigh, the sound of approaching footsteps turned both girls' heads.

Mr. Donner emerged from the thinning crowd, tall and composed, his tie slightly loosened as though the day had barely worn him down. A leather satchel hung from one hand, his rolled-up sleeves slipping toward his wrists. His hazel eyes, sharp and intent, scanned the hallway before settling on them.

"Miss Turner. Miss Lewis." His voice was smooth and calm, but commanded attention.

Katie leaned casually against her locker, a smirk tugging at the corner of her mouth. "Mr. Donner. What's the occasion? Hallway duty, or do you just like hanging out with us delinquents?"

He arched an eyebrow at her, his expression cool but vaguely amused. "Someone has to make sure you all make it out of here in one piece. Especially you, Miss Lewis. I assume you've been using your time wisely today?"

"Define wisely," Katie replied, popping her Bubble Tape with a loud snap.

Lisa bit back a laugh, shifting her bag awkwardly as Mr. Donner turned his attention to her. His expression softened just enough to make her pulse quicken.

"And you, Miss Turner," he said, his tone warmer now. "I trust you've had a more productive day than your friend here?"

Lisa hesitated, caught off guard by the way his eyes lingered on her a moment too long. There was nothing overtly inappropriate, but the way he looked at her left her slightly breathless.

"Uh, yeah. Totally. Redoing the titration experiment three times really...helped drive the point home."

Katie snorted beside her. "Lisa's a perfectionist, Mr. Donner. You should see her notes. They're so color-coded, even Lisa Frank would need sunglasses."

Lisa shot her a glare, her cheeks burning. "Thanks, Katie," she muttered through gritted teeth, then quickly added, "I guess."

Mr. Donner's lips quirked into a small, unreadable smile, his gaze flicking briefly between the two girls before settling back on Lisa.

"Perfectionism is an admirable trait," he said. "Just don't let it become your undoing."

Lisa forced a smile and nodded, wanting to say something but unsure how to respond.

Mr. Donner glanced at the clock above the exit, then back at Katie. "And Miss Lewis, maybe next week you'll actually show up for class. Chemistry isn't optional, no matter how charming you think you are."

Katie grinned, her blue eyes sparkling with mischief. "But it's Friday. Don't we get points for surviving the week?"

"Not in my class," he said, his gaze steady. "You'd do well to remember that."

Katie mock-saluted him. "Yes sir."

Mr. Donner let out a quiet chuckle, shifting the strap of his satchel. "Well, don't let me keep you. Have a good weekend, girls."

As he turned and walked away, Lisa exhaled a breath she hadn't realized she was holding. Katie, of course, was already watching her with a knowing smile.

"God, could you like blush any harder?" Katie teased, her voice low enough not to carry. "I swear, he probably thinks you're writing him love letters in the margins of your lab reports."

"Fuck off!" Lisa snapped, her voice rising a little too much. "He's just...nice. That's all."

Katie gasped in mock horror. "Did Little Miss Virgin just drop an F-bomb?"

Lisa groaned. "You're the worst. Remind me why we're friends again?"

Just then, Tyler jogged up, Nerf ball tucked under his arm. "Hey," he said, kissing Katie's cheek before glancing after Donner. "Was he giving you a hard time again?"

Lisa froze for a half second. Katie shrugged. "Just the usual."

Tyler's jaw tensed. "The guy never seems to turn it off. Like, dude, relax, it's just high school."

Lisa gave a crooked smile. "Maybe he just cares about his students."

"Yeah. Maybe," Tyler said, unconvinced.

He squeezed Katie's arm. "Alright, I'll see you girls later." A quick kiss on her temple, then he jogged off, the Nerf ball bouncing against his hip.

"Anyway," Lisa said, rolling her eyes. "I'm really excited for tonight. My mom left cash for pizza and Blockbuster. I was thinking *The Craft* and *Clueless*."

Lisa's mom had remarried the year before and now disappeared to Napa most weekends, leaving Lisa with pizza money and a strict "no boys" policy.

Katie grinned. "Perfect combo."

As they headed out, Lisa's mind wandered back to Mr. Donner—how his voice seemed deeper when he said her name, how he always met her eyes like he was searching for something. It was ridiculous, she knew. He was her teacher, nothing more.

"Earth to Lisa," Katie's teasing voice cut in. "Are you even listening to me?"

Lisa pushed the thought aside with a shake of her head. He probably didn't even notice her blush, she told herself. Probably.

"Yeah, sorry," she answered.

As they exited through the front door of the school, the late afternoon sun felt warmer than usual, pressing against her back like an unspoken warning. She forced the thought away. Tonight was supposed to be fun.

What could possibly go wrong?

CHAPTER 3

J uniper Falls was a small town nestled between dense forests, with winding backroads that disappeared into the hills. The air carried the fragrant blend of freshly cut grass and a touch of gasoline, emanating from a group of seniors hanging out in the parking lot, the engines of their cars rumbling. The bass of their music thrummed steadily, providing a rebellious counterpoint to the soft chirping of crickets.

Katie waved goodbye to Tyler, who leaned casually against his cherry-red '94 Camaro, one arm slung over the roof, flashing them a grin like he was in a music video.

"You girls need a ride?" he called toward them.

"We're good, thanks!" Lisa hollered back, cupping her hands around her mouth for effect.

"I'll hit you up later then. Maybe I can stop by."

"Girls only, Tyler!" Lisa called back.

"Your loss," he quipped, his voice light with teasing. "But don't call me crying when you run out of snacks."

Katie blew Tyler a kiss, her cheeks flushing slightly. "Drive safe," she called, her voice soft and affectionate.

Tyler caught the invisible kiss with an exaggerated flourish and grinned. "Always do, babe," he replied, giving her a wink before sliding into his car.

As they turned away, Lisa nudged Katie with her elbow. "You're so lucky he likes you," she said sarcastically.

Katie laughed, tossing her hair over her shoulder. "Please. He's lucky I tolerate him. You'd think dating a varsity football player would feel like the movies, but it's mostly sweaty jerseys and way too much Drakkar Noir."

Lisa shook her head. "Wow, so romantic."

A few steps ahead, Ben stood by his bike, unlocking the chain from the rack. He glanced over at them, then back down, clearly trying not to look like he'd been eavesdropping.

Katie nudged Lisa. "There's your lab boyfriend."

Ben looked up then, as if sensing their eyes on him. "Hey, Lisa," he said, lifting a hand. "If you want help with the redo, I'll be in the library before first period on Monday."

Lisa hesitated for half a second, caught off guard. "Uh, sure. Thanks, Ben."

He smiled politely, then hopped on his bike. "Have a good weekend," he called, pedaling off.

The girls watched him disappear down the sidewalk, the quiet whir of his tires swallowed by distance.

Katie gave Lisa a look. "Well, that was very wholesome."

Lisa exhaled through her nose, already walking. "Let's go. I want to hit Blockbuster before the movies are gone."

As they made their way down the sidewalk, they passed Milo's Deli, where a neon sign flickered *Best Hoagies in Town* and the movie theater marquee still displayed last week's showings: *The First Wives Club* and *The Rich Man's Wife*.

"Women married to rich men are really having their moment," Katie said.

"Can I skip the gross man and just take the money?" Lisa replied, brushing a stray hair from her face.

Katie kicked a stray pebble, watching it skitter across the sidewalk before stepping into her path. "Come on, dream big. At least marry the guy before you take him for everything."

Lisa rolled her eyes and veered around her, quickening her pace as the breeze picked up, the glow of the marquee fading behind them.

As they walked further into town, the blue-and-yellow Blockbuster sign beckoned. Inside, the scent of popcorn and plastic VHS cases filled the air, accompanied by the steady hum of an overhead fan. A cardboard standee of *Twister* stood at the entrance, its edges slightly frayed from months of wear.

"I swear, if even one of the movies are checked out, I'm suing for emotional distress," Katie declared, marching straight toward the *New Releases* section.

Lisa giggled, trailing behind. "We could always get *Hocus Pocus* as a backup. Even darker than *The Craft*, despite its rating, and full of sisterly love amongst the mayhem."

Katie stopped mid-stride and gave Lisa a mock-serious glare. "*Hocus Pocus* is a masterpiece, but tonight is about teenage angst and rebellion, not campy broomstick choreography."

Lisa held up her hands in surrender, grinning. "Fair enough."

Katie resumed her march, weaving between aisles like a woman on a mission. "If we don't find *The Craft*, I'm blaming you for jinxing us with that backup nonsense."

Reaching the *New Releases* section, Katie scanned the shelves with laser focus, her fingers skimming the spines of the VHS cases. When she spotted the familiar cover of *The Craft*, she snatched it up triumphantly and held it up like a trophy.

Lisa clapped her hands together. "Crisis averted. Emotional distress lawsuit canceled. And look, they even have *Clueless*," she said as she grabbed the last copy.

Katie grinned and handed Lisa the tape in her hand. "Now, let's grab snacks and get the hell out of this horrible lighting." She steered them toward the candy display, grabbing a handful of candy with a flourish. "Perfect," Katie declared, as if she'd solved an unsolvable mystery.

Lisa glanced at Katie's selections. "You're really going all out, huh?"

Katie smirked, picking up a pack of M&Ms. "Movie nights require commitment. We're building memories here, Lisa."

"We've got everything we need for a perfect night: girl power, witchcraft, and the unparalleled wisdom of Cher Horowitz, aka Emma Woodhouse" Lisa said.

"Who?" Katie asked.

"Emma Woodhouse. Jane Austen?" Lisa said.

"No clue."

"Nevermind."

The girls waited in line behind a pair of middle school boys loudly arguing with their mom, who refused to let them rent an R-rated horror movie with a chainsaw on the cover. One of them tried to claim it was "historical," which only earned him a death glare and a firm *absolutely not*.

When the family finally shuffled off, the clerk, a bored-looking guy in his early twenties with a *Soundgarden* T-shirt, glanced up from behind the counter and gave a barely perceptible nod. "Next."

Katie stepped forward, nudging Lisa with her elbow. The clerk raised an eyebrow as he scanned their tapes. "Solid chick flicks," he said flatly, barely looking up.

Katie grinned, nodding. "Wait! We forgot the popcorn."

Lisa sighed, shaking her head with a small smile. "I've got it." She grabbed two bags of microwave popcorn from the display near the counter and handed them over, fishing a crumpled bill from her pocket to cover it.

The clerk gave a half-smile as he bagged their items. "Enjoy your curated chaos or whatever."

Katie grabbed the bag and winked. "Oh, we will. Rock on, *Soundgarden*."

As they stepped into the cool late afternoon air, the Blockbuster sign flickered to life above them. The sun was beginning to sink behind the hills, casting long shadows across the parking lot. Katie clutched their movie night treasures while Lisa fell into step beside her, both girls grinning with the anticipation that only comes from a perfect Friday night stretching ahead, completely unaware that by morning, everything would be different.

CHAPTER 4

Lisa and Katie crossed the Blockbuster parking lot toward the street, Katie digging through the candy bag, when a car door slammed behind them.

"Hey, losers," came a familiar voice.

They both turned.

Tyler leaned against his cherry-red Camaro, arms folded, his varsity jacket slung casually over one shoulder. His smirk was pure 80s heartthrob, cocky, deliberate, like he'd been rehearsing that line in the mirror all afternoon.

Katie blinked. "What the hell? How long have you been here?"

He shrugged. "Long enough to watch you agonize over the candy like your lives depended on it."

Lisa narrowed her eyes. "Were you spying on us?"

"I would've paged you," Tyler said, "but seeing as none of us live in a teen soap or own a pager, I figured I'd go full old-school stalker instead."

Katie snorted. "What, just lurking in the shadows of Blockbuster like some kind of denim-clad phantom?"

He grinned. "Phantom of the VHS aisle. Coming soon to a theater near you."

Lisa shook her head and slid into the backseat. "You're both so dumb."

"Dumb," Katie said, slinging her bag into the front seat, "but charming. And really good at sex. That's why I keep him around."

Tyler slid behind the wheel and glanced at Katie as he turned the key. "That and the free rides."

Lisa sighed and reached for her seatbelt, but Tyler pulled away before she could snap it into place.

As they cruised through the neighborhood, a moody Alanis Morissette ballad drifted from the speakers. Tyler tapped the steering wheel in time with the beat, then shot a glance at Katie out of the corner of his eye.

"So...no chance I'm crashing the party tonight?" Tyler asked.

Katie hesitated, chewing her gum a little slower. "It's girls-only. You know the drill."

Lisa jumped in. "My mom's rule, not mine."

Tyler held up both hands. "All good. Just figured I'd ask. Can't blame a guy for wanting to be part of *The Craft* and *Clueless* double-feature."

Katie smirked. "You just want to braid our hair and talk about boys."

He grinned. "Only if we can paint our nails too."

Tyler pulled into Lisa's driveway. The porch light flicked on automatically, casting their shadows long across the grass.

Katie leaned over and kissed Tyler's cheek. "Thanks for the ride, stalker."

"Anytime."

Lisa hesitated before getting out. "Thanks, Tyler. Seriously."

Lisa got out of the car, walked up the steps and disappeared inside, the screen door creaking shut behind her.

Katie lingered by the car, one foot still on the pavement. Tyler stayed in the driver's seat, both hands on the wheel like he wasn't sure if he should leave or wait.

For a second, they just looked at each other.

"You okay?" he asked finally, his voice low.

Katie nodded. "Yeah. I'll just miss you."

"I wasn't trying to crash the night or anything. I know it's your thing—Lisa, movies, the whole girl power ritual or whatever."

Katie smiled, but there was a flicker of guilt for wanting Tyler there, even though tonight was supposed to be just her and Lisa.

"I know Lisa will kill me for this, but you can come by later if you want. Like much later."

Tyler raised an eyebrow. "You can count on it."

Katie leaned in and kissed his cheek again. He smiled, but it didn't quite reach his eyes.

"Any chance I'll get lucky?" he teased.

"Not even a little."

She backed away from the car, hands tucked into the sleeves of her flannel. "Drive safe, okay?"

Tyler watched her until she stepped onto the porch and opened the front door.

Just before she slipped inside, she glanced back.

"Love you."

Then she closed the door.

Tyler sat there longer than he meant to, watching the porch light illuminate the empty driveway. Something felt off—maybe it was the way the shadows seemed deeper tonight, or how quiet the street was for a Friday evening. Finally, he shifted into drive, but kept checking his rearview mirror as he pulled away.

The light stayed on, growing smaller, until he rounded the bend and lost sight of it.

Chapter 5

By the time both girls were inside, the sun had dipped lower in the sky, casting long shadows over the quiet street. The neighborhood was sparsely lined with houses, each set far apart, their wide front yards separated by stretches of overgrown hedges and open spaces.

The house was a neat, two-story colonial with white shutters and a tire swing swaying gently from an old oak tree in the front yard. From a distance, it looked like something out of a brochure—almost too perfect—but up close the paint was beginning to peel, and the swing's rope was frayed with age. Crickets filled the stillness with their steady chirping, broken now and then by the dry rustle of leaves in the evening breeze.

Inside, the air smelled faintly of lavender and the lingering sweetness of freshly baked cookies, courtesy of Lisa's mom, who always left a stash before heading out of town. Lisa immediately kicked off her white canvas Skechers Roadies, their thick rubber soles thudding against the hardwood, and motioned for Katie to do the same.

Katie flopped onto the couch and stretched out dramatically. "Let the sleepover of the century commence!"

Lisa rolled her eyes but smiled. "You always say that."

"Because it's always true."

It was routine now. The pizza order, the Blockbuster tapes, the quiz magazines, and the endless bags of candy. But the comfort of it all, the way the night unfolded in predictable waves, was something neither of them ever said aloud but both depended on.

They'd been having sleepovers since they were eight, since Katie's mom had first started working nights and Lisa's parents were still together. Back then, they'd shared twin beds, made friendship bracelets out of yarn, and whispered about the kids in their class they hated or loved.

Katie remembered one night in sixth grade, when Lisa had woken up crying. Her dad had missed her birthday. She'd tried to hide it, but Katie saw the card on the floor, unopened. No gift. Just a scribbled signature and a $10 bill.

Katie hadn't said anything then. Just got up, pulled out the glitter pens, and made a new card with her. "You don't need him," she'd said. "You've got me."

Lisa had nodded. Wiped her eyes. And they'd watched *My Girl* for the third time that month.

Even now, so much older, it still felt like the rest of the world couldn't reach them when they were here, cocooned in blankets and late-night sugar highs.

Lisa walked into the kitchen, grabbing the cordless phone off the counter. "What do you want on the pizza? Pepperoni? Mushrooms?"

Katie made a face. "Mushrooms are a fungus. Why would you ruin pizza like that?"

Lisa sighed. "Fine. Half pepperoni, half plain cheese. You're so picky." She dialed the number from memory, her fingers pressing the oversized buttons.

Katie called out from the living room. "And breadsticks! Don't forget the breadsticks. I'm a growing girl."

Lisa laughed as the line connected. "Hi Mr. Moretti. It's Lisa on Corsica Lane. Can I get a large pizza, half pepperoni, half cheese, an order of breadsticks, and a two-liter of Coke?"

"Diet coke," Katie called from the living room.

"Make that a Diet Coke, Mr. Moretti. And three bottles, please. Yeah, that's it. Thanks!"

Lisa hung up and walked back into the living room, where Katie had already claimed the remote and was flipping through channels. "Pizza's on its way."

"Great. I'm starving," Katie said, landing on *MTV*. The faint strains of *Wannabe* by the Spice Girls filled the room as the video started to play on screen. "Ugh, this song has been out for months and it's still *every-where*," Katie said, but she hummed along anyway.

Lisa dropped onto the couch beside her and pulled her knees up. "It's a bop, and you know it."

Katie smirked. "Fine, but if we're gonna dance to it, I'm gonna be Scary Spice. You can have Sporty."

Lisa caught the throw pillow Katie tossed at her. "Deal. But only if you promise not to butcher the accent. And that no one finds out we dance to the Spice Girls."

They jumped up in unison as the chorus hit, launching into their choreographed routine like they'd rehearsed it for a world tour. Pillow in one hand, invisible mic in the other, they spun, kicked, and lip-synced with wild abandon. They knew every word, every move, and exactly when to drop to the floor during the bridge.

They collapsed onto the couch in a heap of laughter, breathless and glowing, the last notes of the song fading into the hum of the next music video.

By the time the TV rolled into a commercial break nearly thirty minutes later, both girls jumped up again at the sound of the doorbell. Katie darted to the entry-way and yanked it open.

She blinked.

"...Ben?"

Ben stood on the porch in a too-big red Crestfield Pizza windbreaker, clutching the pizza box like it might fall apart in his hands. His eyes darted from Katie to Lisa, then back down to the receipt stapled to the box.

"Oh. Uh, hey," he said, avoiding eye contact. "Large half pepperoni, half cheese, breadsticks, and three Cokes?"

"Diet cokes," Katie said.

Ben looked down in the bag with the sodas.

"Diet cokes," he corrected.

"That's us," Lisa said, smiling.

Ben held out the receipt, fumbling slightly with the pen clipped to the top. "It's, um...thirteen seventy-five."

Katie pulled a crumpled twenty from her pocket and handed it over. "Keep the change."

Ben's ears went red. "Oh, uh, thanks."

Katie took the pizza box, the warmth seeping into her hands. Lisa reached for the breadsticks and drinks, careful not to drop anything.

"Your lab partner delivers pizza. That's so cute," Katie teased, nudging Lisa with her elbow.

Lisa gave a mock glare but couldn't hide her grin. "Thanks, Ben. See you later."

Ben nodded too quickly. "Yeah. Okay. Bye."

He turned, then stumbled slightly on the step before catching himself and hurrying off toward his car.

Katie shut the door slowly, grinning. "I think he blushed."

"He always blushes," Lisa said, walking back to the couch with her arms full. "It's like his default setting."

"Still," Katie said, placing the pizza on the coffee table. "That was kind of adorable."

Lisa plopped down beside her, opening the breadsticks and taking a whiff. "Dinner of champions."

They settled back onto the couch, the music videos resuming in the background.

"Movie time!" Katie announced as they set the food down on the coffee table.

Lisa held up *The Craft* and handed it to her. "I'm so excited to watch these again.

Katie loaded the VHS into the player, grabbed the VCR remote and joined Lisa on the floor.

They sat cross-legged, eating pizza and laughing at how dramatic the spells in *The Craft* seemed. "If we called the corners, we'd probably accidentally summon the ghost of your grandma who'd yell at us for eating on the carpet," Katie joked.

By the time the credits rolled, both girls were more relaxed, their giggles filling the room as Katie swapped the tape for *Clueless*.

CHAPTER 6

The twilight sky cast a soft, orange glow over the quiet street as Evelyn Winslow tugged on the leash of her elderly terrier, Buster. The dog shuffled along beside her, his movements slow and deliberate. Evelyn clicked her tongue impatiently.

"Come on, Buster, we don't have all night," she muttered, pulling her light jacket tighter against the crisp autumn air. A faint scent of damp leaves and woodsmoke lingered, a hallmark of the season in their suburban enclave.

The houses on their street were spaced generously apart, separated by sprawling lawns and clusters of old oaks. Evelyn preferred it that way. It gave her room to breathe, to think, and, of course, to keep an eye on her neighbors.

Buster stopped abruptly, sniffing at a patch of grass near the sidewalk. Evelyn sighed, letting her gaze wander to the Turner house, about fifty yards down the street. She noticed the lights were on, and movement inside caught her attention.

Lisa Turner and her purple-haired friend were bustling around, their silhouettes visible through the living room window. Evelyn pursed her lips. "Looks like the girls are having another one of their little sleepovers," she murmured to Buster. "And with no adult supervision, no less."

Buster let out a half-hearted sneeze, tugging at the leash again.

Evelyn's sharp eyes scanned the rest of the street. Most of the houses were dark, their occupants likely tucked in for the night or glued to their TVs.

She lingered a moment longer, her gaze flicking back to the window. The girls were laughing, one of them triumphantly sinking her teeth into a greasy pizza.

Evelyn sighed. She wasn't one to meddle, well, not much, but something about the Turner house always put her on edge. Maybe it was the way the girl's mom left her alone so often, or maybe it was just the nagging feeling that trouble had a way of finding teenagers with too much freedom.

"Let's go, Buster," she said, giving the leash a gentle tug.

As she turned toward home, Evelyn cast one last glance over her shoulder at the Turner house. The laughter inside seemed louder now, drifting through the stillness of the street. She tightened her grip on Buster's leash, a faint scowl crossing her face.

"Mark my words," she muttered under her breath, "nothing good ever comes out of nights like these."

She shivered slightly, though whether from the faint chill or the uneasy feeling prickling at the back of her neck, she couldn't say.

Chapter 7

Eric's knuckles were white against the shovel's rough handle. His flashlight, balanced on a nearby rock, threw jagged shadows across the forest floor as he worked. The silence pressed against his ears. It was the kind of deep quiet that made every breath sound too loud.

He'd driven for miles beyond the edge of town, past where pavement cracked into gravel, where gravel dissolved into dirt tracks that hardly qualified as roads. The woods swallowed what little moonlight pierced the canopy, leaving him with nothing but the smell of damp earth and rotting leaves.

And the sickening knowledge of what waited in the car's trunk.

Two bodies. Still warm when he'd loaded them in.

Eric hadn't looked at them since loading them into the tarp. He couldn't. Even now, the metallic tang of blood clung to his nostrils, no matter how often he rubbed at his face or spat on the ground to clear the taste.

He turned back to the shallow grave he'd been digging, his chest heaving. It wasn't deep enough. Not yet. He stabbed the shovel into the soil again, the dull *thunk* of metal against dirt the only sound breaking the oppressive quiet.

I didn't mean to do it, he told himself, over and over, like a mantra. *It was an accident.*

But he couldn't unsee the way Matt had crumpled to the ground, the blood pooling around his head like a grotesque halo. He couldn't unhear the scream that had erupted from Laura's throat as she lunged at him, her nails tearing across his face.

Eric paused, leaning on the shovel as he stared into the dark pit. He wiped the sweat from his brow with a trembling hand, smearing dirt across his forehead. It wasn't supposed to end like this. He'd gone to the house to confront Laura and Matt, to demand answers, to maybe throw a punch or two. But now...

Now he was here, burying their bodies in the middle of nowhere, like a coward.

The crunch of leaves behind him sent his heart into his throat. He spun around, his flashlight casting erratic beams into the trees, catching nothing but tangled branches and leaves. The woods were dark and unyielding. He let out a shaky breath and turned back to the grave.

You're losing it, he thought. *Get it done and get out of here.*

With renewed urgency, Eric grabbed the edge of the tarp and dragged it from the truck bed. The weight of it nearly toppled him, but he steadied himself, gritting his teeth as he maneuvered it closer to the hole. His breath came in sharp bursts, his muscles screaming with the effort.

The tarp unfolded slightly as it hit the ground, revealing a pale, bloodied hand. Eric recoiled instinctively, his stomach lurching. He stumbled back, his foot catching on the edge of the shovel. He hit the ground hard, the air knocked from his lungs.

For a moment, he just lay there, staring up at the dark canopy of trees.

"Get up," he muttered to himself. "Get up and finish this."

He pushed himself to his feet, avoiding the exposed hand as he grabbed the tarp and shoved it toward the edge of the grave. With one final heave, the bodies slid into the pit, landing with a sickening thud that echoed in his ears.

Eric stared down at them, his chest tight. They looked small in the hole, almost insignificant. But the weight of what he'd done pressed down on him, heavier than any shovel or tarp.

He grabbed the shovel and began covering them, the dirt falling in heavy clumps. Each scoop felt like it took a piece of him with it, burying his life along with theirs.

When the grave was full, he flattened the dirt with the back of the shovel, trying to make the ground look undisturbed. He gathered fallen leaves and scattered them over the fresh soil, his hands trembling.

Finally, he wiped the blade of the shovel with a handful of dry grass and tossed it into the bed of his truck, the clatter echoing through the silent woods.

Eric turned off the flashlight, plunging everything into darkness. He stood there for a moment, his breath fogging in the cold air, his heart pounding in the silence. Then he climbed into Laura's car and started the engine, the roar breaking the eerie stillness. He would figure out how to get rid of it tomorrow.

As he drove away, he glanced in the rearview mirror, just a reflex, but froze. For a split second, he saw them. Standing at the edge of the trees. Watching. Then he blinked, and they were gone. Just the trees again, standing like silent sentinels over his terrible secret.

He began to relax once he was sure he wasn't being followed.

CHAPTER 8

The screen flickered with the final scene of *Clueless*, Cher and Josh finally together as the credits rolled. Katie lounged on her stomach, a slice of half-eaten pizza cooling on a paper plate in front of her.

"Ugh, Paul Rudd is so cute," Lisa said, sprawled on the floor under a blanket. She popped a Sour Patch Kid into her mouth.

Katie snorted, eyes still on the TV. "He's, like, aggressively decent. That's his whole charm."

Lisa threw a pillow at her. "He's got that broody, intellectual vibe. He looks like he'll never age. Admit it, you'd marry him in a heartbeat."

"Only if I got to keep Cher's wardrobe," Katie shot back, dodging the pillow and stuffing a piece of crust into her mouth.

Lisa reached for the remote and turned off the TV. "Okay, now what? Should I prepare for Tyler crashing the party and demanding a pillow fight, or are we painting our nails?"

Katie rolled onto her back, wiggling her fingers in the air. "Nails, duh. I want those perfect French tips you never shut up about."

Lisa grinned and reached toward the coffee table, pulling a mini nail polish kit from the drawer. "I was hoping you'd say that."

They spent the next half hour in a haze of nail polish fumes and giggles, the coffee table strewn with open bottles and stray cotton balls. Katie picked out a dark purple, while Lisa went for bright pink.

By the time their nails dried, they were lying on the floor, flipping through a stack of magazines. Lisa waved the latest issue of *Cosmopolitan* in Katie's face, turning to the quiz section with a grin. "Wanna find out if you're actually as smooth as you think?"

Katie rolled her eyes but grabbed the magazine anyway. "Please. I already know I'm effortlessly charming."

She flipped to the first question and read it aloud in a dramatic voice. "When you spot your crush, what's your move? A) Flash him a killer smile that says 'I'm confident but not desperate' - hello, major flirt alert!, B) Do the casual arm-brush while grabbing your lipgloss - totally accidental, right?, C) Scribble his initials plus yours in your day planner like some lovesick puppy, or D) Go into total shutdown mode because showing feelings is basically social death?"

Lisa pushed her glasses up her nose and laughed. "D. Definitely D."

"I'm a textbook A," Katie beamed.

Lisa nodded. "That you are."

They dissolved into laughter as they took turns answering the ridiculous questions, their late-night chatter filling the quiet house.

Outside, the night seemed to listen, waiting.

CHAPTER 9

Eric's hands trembled against the steering wheel, his fingers readjusting their grip every few seconds as if the wheel might slip away. The car tore through the winding backroads, the headlights barely cutting through the oppressive darkness of the forest. The air inside smelled like wet dirt, sweat, and something faintly metallic—blood, maybe, though he wasn't sure if it was real or just in his head.

His shirt clung to his back, soaked through with panic. The shovel had bounced around in the trunk earlier, every metallic clatter a gunshot in his mind, until he stopped to wedge it between the seats. Now it lay there, mocking him, its dirty handle within arm's reach.

He couldn't stop thinking about the shallow graves, the way the earth resisted his every desperate shove. His boots had sunk into the mud, making him feel like the earth itself wanted to drag him down.

The faces wouldn't leave him alone, either. Matt's pale, lifeless eyes stared at him every time he blinked, and Laura—*God, Laura*—she had gone down too easy.

And then, cutting through the chaos in his mind, a softer image surfaced: Ellie. His daughter. The thought of her had slipped in before he could stop it, and now it wouldn't leave.

Ellie was probably asleep in her dorm room right now, a few hundred miles away. He could picture the way she'd hugged him goodbye just a few weeks ago, her arms tight around his neck.

"I'll call you all the time, Dad," she'd promised, her voice soft but steady, just like her mother's.

He'd stood on the curb watching her drive away, his chest tight with an ache he couldn't explain. Ellie had always been his light, the one thing he'd managed to get right in a life filled with wrong turns. She was so damn smart, too—studying pre-med, planning to save lives. If she ever found out about tonight, about what he'd done...

His grip on the steering wheel tightened. She wouldn't find out. No one would. He'd make sure of that.

"Pull it together," he muttered to himself, shaking his head. His voice sounded alien, too loud in the confined space of the car.

He checked the rearview mirror for the hundredth time. Empty. Still empty. But that didn't mean anything, did it? It was too quiet out here, the kind of quiet that felt alive. Every shadow between the trees seemed to shift and lean toward the road, reaching for him.

The radio crackled faintly, an old pop song playing just low enough to be unnerving. He reached for the knob to turn it off, but his hand trembled too much, and he yanked it back. His fingers drummed against the steering wheel instead, the rhythm frantic, uneven.

In the distance, the road curved sharply. He took the turn too fast, the tires skidding slightly on the loose gravel before gripping again. The car fishtailed, and for a second, his stomach dropped like a stone.

He slammed his fist against the wheel, shouting, "Get it together, damn it!"

The anger helped, even if only for a moment. He forced his breathing to slow, counting silently in his head. One, two, three. In through the nose, out through the mouth. His therapist's voice echoed faintly in his memory.

Center yourself, Eric. You can't control everything, but you can control your reaction.

Right. Center himself. Like that was possible now.

The lights of a small town flickered faintly on the horizon. Civilization. Safety. He just had to get home, clean up, and pretend none of this ever happened. Once he got rid of Laura's car, of course. He could do that. He *would* do that. He had no other choice.

But then, there it was. The flash of red and blue in the rearview mirror.

"No," he whispered, his stomach twisting into knots. "Fuck! Fuck! Fuck!"

The cruiser came up fast, its headlights blinding. The siren let out a single wail, a sharp warning that sent a jolt of ice down his spine.

Eric eased off the gas, his mind racing as he tried to come up with an excuse, a story, anything that might save him.

His hands were shaking as he pulled the car to the side of the road. The cruiser stopped behind him, its lights strobing in the darkness.

"Calm down," he muttered, his voice barely a whisper. "It's gonna be okay."

The crunch of boots on gravel drew closer. He could see the silhouette of the officer in his side mirror, his flashlight beam cutting through the night like a scalpel.

Eric wiped his hands on his pants, leaving streaks of mud on the fabric. His mouth felt dry as sandpaper. When the flashlight tapped against the window, he rolled it down, forcing a shaky smile onto his face.

"Evenin', officer," he said, his voice cracking.

The cop's sharp eyes scanned him, then the interior of the car. Eric could feel the weight of that gaze, the unspoken questions it carried. He tried not to flinch when the officer's beam landed on the handle of the shovel poking out from the backseat.

"What's the rush tonight?" the cop asked, his tone even but probing.

Eric opened his mouth, but no words came out. His thoughts were a tangle of panic and half-formed lies.

"License and registration," the cop said, his eyes narrowing.

Eric fumbled for the documents, knowing this moment could either save him or doom him. The shovel and pickaxe sat like ticking time bombs in his periphery, and he couldn't stop thinking about the dirt under his nails and the faint trace of blood he swore he could still smell.

And when the officer leaned closer, his flashlight catching the faint streaks of dirt on Eric's sleeve, he knew the clock had run out.

CHAPTER 10

L isa yawned, stretching her arms above her head. "Okay, my nails are dry, I'm stuffed, and officially out of magazines. What's next?"

Katie glanced at the clock on the VCR, the glowing numbers reading *11:47 PM*. She grinned, a mischievous sparkle in her eye. "Wanna do something fun?"

Lisa rolled onto her side, narrowing her eyes. "Define *fun*.

Katie reached for the phone on the coffee table, twirling the cord around her finger. "Prank calls. Like, the most essential sleepover activity ever. It's practically illegal not to do them."

Lisa, sprawled on the carpet with a bag of Doritos, snorted. "What are we, twelve? Besides, no one will even answer their phone this late."

Katie waved her off. "Trust me, it'll be hilarious. It's either this or watching *Girls Gone Wild* commercials until we pass out from all the sugar and carbs."

She got up, snatching the thick city phone book from the shelf by the TV. Holding it up like a trophy, she grinned. "Let's see who's worthy of making our call list."

Lisa groaned but sat up, licking orange dust from her fingers. "Fine. But if someone's grandma picks up, we're hanging up immediately. No exceptions."

Katie smirked, flipping the phone book open. "Relax, I've got this." She ran her finger down the page with an exaggerated flair before stopping at a random number. Before dialing, she punched in *67, glancing at Lisa with a wink. "Anonymous, baby."

Lisa rolled her eyes but couldn't hide her smile.

Katie dialed. The girls stifled their giggles as the line rang. When a groggy voice answered, she barely kept it together. "Hi, this is Linda from the cable company. We noticed you've been ordering a lot of porn on Pay-Per-View. Should we just go ahead and put you on the monthly subscription plan? It comes with a free trial of Skinamax."

"Is that really an option? I'd be interested." The man on the line said.

The girls exploded into laughter as Katie hung up the phone. Lisa collapsed back onto the carpet, scrunching her nose. "Ew, men are disgusting."

"I don't know. I find the storylines on Skinamax quite interesting," Katie said and laughed.

"Gross," Lisa said as Katie passed her the phone. "Your turn," she said.

Lisa groaned but reluctantly grabbed the receiver, nervously flipping through the phone book. "Okay, okay. But what am I even supposed to say? I'm totally gonna mess this up."

She stopped at a random name, then looked at Katie with wide, panicked eyes.

"You're gonna rock this!" Katie cheered her on. "Don't forget to *67," she reminded her.

Lisa nodded and dialed, clearing her throat nervously.

A man's voice answered with a groggy "hello" and Lisa suddenly switched into a super peppy, radio-DJ voice. "Hi! This is...Tracy from 94.7 Hot Hits FM.

Congratulations, you've just won two VIP tickets to see the Spice Girls live in concert!"

There was a pause, then the voice asked: "Wait...what?"

Lisa kept going, all business. "That's right! You and a guest will enjoy front-row seats, backstage access, and a private meet-and-greet with the Girls. All you have to do is answer our final trivia question to claim your prize. Are you ready?"

The guy hesitated. "Uh...I didn't enter anything. And isn't it too late for a call like this?"

Katie nudged Lisa, mouthing keep going.

Lisa didn't miss a beat. "Oh, don't worry! This is a random giveaway for our loyal listeners. Your number was pulled from our listener line. Now, for the question: What's the name of the debut Spice Girls album?"

A long pause. Then, finally, the guy mumbled, "Uh... Spice?"

Lisa clapped a hand over the receiver, pretending to announce it to a crowd. "And we have a WINNER of the 'Wannabe' experience package. You'll get to slam your body down and zig-a-zig-ah with the Girls backstage. Now all we need from you is-" Lisa stopped mid-sentence, hung up the phone and collapsed onto the floor, wheezing.

Katie wiped away tears of laughter. "That was so messed up. You were great. I knew you had it in you."

Lisa gasped for air. "Okay that was a total rush. More?"

Katie grabbed the phone book. "Obviously."

Katie flipped through the phone book with wild abandon, one leg draped over the arm of the couch, eyes gleaming with mischief. "Okay, next victim. I'm thinking someone with a majorly boring name. Like...Dale. That name is so 'I wear pocket protectors and work at the DMV.'"

Lisa snorted, sprawled out on the floor surrounded by Sour Patch Kids wrappers. "Poor Dale. He didn't ask for this."

Katie paused, then grinned. "Actually, you know who you should call?"

Lisa looked up, already wary. "Please don't say it."

"Mr. Donner." Katie waggled her eyebrows. "Tell him you need help with extra credit...heavy on the chemistry."

Lisa sat up straighter, her expression immediately shifting. "That's not funny."

Katie blinked. "Okay. It was just a joke."

Lisa busied herself by turning pages in the phone book. "Yeah, well. It's still not funny."

Katie's teasing grin faltered for just a second before she leaned back, trying to play it off. "Okay, okay. Switching gears. Sorry, Miss Sensitive."

Lisa didn't look up. "Just pick a new number."

Katie nodded and pointed to a random number. But the energy in the room had shifted a bit. Enough to leave a crack.

Lisa kept her eyes on the phonebook, but her face was a little redder than before.

And Katie noticed. For the first time that night, the laughter felt a little forced.

She didn't say anything more about it.

CHAPTER 11

T he flashlight beam stayed fixed on Eric's sleeve, the streaks of mud glaring back at him like a spotlight on his guilt. Eric squinted at the officer's chest, making out the nametag in the harsh light—*Harrington*.

The officer's face was unreadable, his eyes narrowing as though he was trying to piece together a puzzle.

"Step out of the car," Harrington said, his voice calm but commanding.

Eric froze. His body screamed at him to move, to obey, but his mind was racing through a dozen terrible outcomes. None of them ended with him going home tonight. None of them ended with him free.

"Officer, I—" Eric started, his voice shaky.

"Now," Harrington barked, his hand drifting toward his holstered weapon. The cop's eyes flicked toward the backseat, where the shovel's wooden handle jutted out like evidence waiting to testify.

Eric nodded, his hand trembling as he reached for the door handle.

Ellie's face flashed in his mind, smiling up at him on her first day of college. She'd hugged him tight and said, "I'll make you proud, Dad." He couldn't let her hear about this. He couldn't let it all fall apart.

Harrington took a step back, the flashlight beam never wavering. "Hands where I can see them," he ordered.

Eric hesitated for a moment, then pushed the door open slowly. He slid out of the car, his heart pounding as he raised his hands. The night air was sharp and cold, biting at his skin. Harrington gestured for him to step to the side of the car.

"You've got mud on your clothes, a shovel in your backseat, and you're sweating like a guy running from something," Harrington said, his tone tight. "You want to explain that?"

Eric forced a laugh, but it sounded hollow. "That's easy. I'm a landscaper, sir. Got called out late for an emergency job. Tree roots were threatening a foundation. Took longer than expected, and I guess I look the part."

Harrington didn't buy it. "Turn around. Hands on the hood."

Eric swallowed hard, his body tensing. His eyes flicked toward the cop's holster, then to the cruiser parked behind them. The red and blue lights strobed through the trees, casting shadows that twisted and danced.

"Let's not make this worse than it has to be," Harrington said, stepping closer.

Eric nodded, slowly turning to face the car. His hands rested on the hood, his fingers splayed against the cold metal. His breath came in shallow gasps as Harrington moved behind him.

The sound of the cop's radio crackling made Eric flinch. Harrington paused, one hand reaching for the cuffs on his belt.

This was it. His moment.

In one swift motion, Eric twisted, swinging his elbow back and catching Harrington in the face. The cop stumbled, his flashlight clattering to the ground as he cursed. Eric didn't give him a chance to recover. He lunged forward, grabbing for Harrington's revolver, but Harrington's grip held firm, keeping the weapon out of reach.

The two men grappled, their bodies slamming against the side of the car. Harrington was stronger than he looked, his grip like iron as he tried to wrestle Eric down. But Eric had desperation on his side. He managed to shove the cop back, slamming him into the doorframe.

"Stop!" Harrington shouted, his voice cut off as Eric's hand reached for Harrington's holster. Without thinking, he grabbed the revolver and pressed it against Harrington's chest. For a split second, their eyes met, and Eric saw the realization dawn in the cop's face.

"Please, don't-" Harrington pleaded.

The gunshot was deafening in the stillness of the night. Harrington staggered back, his hand clutching at the spreading dark stain on his shirt. He sank to his knees, his mouth opening and closing as though he wanted to say something.

He couldn't leave the body there.

Still clutching the gun, he staggered forward and crouched beside the deputy, slipping his hands under Harrington's arms. The body was heavier than he expected, solid and slack. He dragged it into the brush, the utility belt catching on roots. The deputy's radio tumbled loose and landed in the weeds.

Eric kicked it deeper into the undergrowth without looking. He rolled Harrington into it and scraped a cover of dead leaves and broken branches over the body. The makeshift burial wouldn't hold up to real scrutiny—even in the dark, anyone looking closely would see the shape beneath—but it might be enough to buy him time. Hopefully.

He stood over the body for a long second, breathing hard. "You should've just walked away," he whispered.

He thought of Ellie again, and the lie he'd have to tell her if he ever saw her again. Then he turned to the cruiser.

He wiped the door handle clean with the edge of his sleeve and climbed in, shifting the car into neutral. Guiding it carefully down a nearby embankment, he let it roll until it was mostly obscured by trees. Not perfect, but better than leaving it in plain sight. He turned off the car and tossed the keys deep into the underbrush, listening to them clatter through the leaves before they disappeared into the dark.

His hand lingered on the steering wheel. Fingerprints.

Eric yanked off the hoodie tied around his waist and used it to wipe down the wheel, the gearshift, the door. He hadn't worn gloves. Of course he hadn't. This wasn't supposed to happen.

He stepped back, staring at the cruiser one last time, then jogged to Laura's car. His hands shook as he tossed the gun onto the passenger seat, slid behind the wheel, and jammed the key into the ignition.

The engine roared to life, loud and jarring against the quiet. He started driving and didn't look back. The road ahead stretched out. Endless, empty. His knuckles ached from how tightly he gripped the wheel. Harrington's face stayed with him, fixed in that final moment, when the light had gone out of his eyes.

Eric blinked hard, trying to focus on the lines in the road. The rhythm of the tires. The silence pressed in, thick and airless, as though the night itself wanted to crush him.

Headlights appeared in the distance. For a moment, he considered jerking the wheel. Letting it end in a blur of glass and metal and silence.

But he didn't. Instead, he adjusted his grip, wiped the sweat from his brow, and kept driving.

He had to go home and pack. Because there was no turning back now.

Chapter 12

For Katie and Lisa, the night unfolded in a blur of absurd calls, fake accents, nonsensical questions, and increasingly ridiculous scenarios. But as the clock crept past midnight, Lisa stifled a yawn.

"Okay, I'm beat," Lisa said. "Maybe we should call it a night."

Katie's grin turned a little sharper.

"Or we can do one more and spice it up," she said, her voice dropping into a conspiratorial whisper. "Say something...creepy."

Lisa hesitated, her fingers hovering over the keypad. "Creepy how?"

Katie's smile widened. "I don't know, something like…we know your secret. I saw it in an old movie once. It'll freak them out."

Lisa raised an eyebrow but couldn't suppress a grin. "You're evil."

"And you love it," Katie replied, nudging her. "Come on, last call. I swear."

Lisa sighed, picking a random number from the phonebook.

Lisa sighed and flipped through the phonebook. "Oh goodie. Another Dale," she said, landing on Dale Mitchell. She dialed *67, then the number.

As the phone rang, the air in the room grew heavier, the earlier laughter fading into an expectant hush.

When someone finally answered, Lisa took a deep breath and whispered, changing her voice as much as she could. "Is this Dale?"

"Yeah? Who's this? Do you know what time it is?"

"We know your secret," she said softly.

The pause on the other end was longer than it should've been.

"Who the fuck is this?" the voice barked, sharp, uneasy.

Lisa's smile faltered. She hung up quickly.

Katie let out a laugh, but it came out a little forced. "Okay, that was pretty good. You've got the creep factor down, but your delivery could be better."

Lisa stared at the phone, a strange prickle creeping up the back of her neck. "That felt...wrong." Then she flopped back onto the couch.

"We can't stop now!" Katie said.

"You said that was the last call."

"We can do better," Katie insisted, already reaching for the phone.

Lisa hesitated. "Are we sure we should keep going? It's super late. What if someone calls the cops?"

Katie grinned, snatching the receiver. "Oh please. This is an art form. Watch and learn." She pressed *67 then dialed a number from the phonebook.

"Hello?" a groggy female voice answered on the second ring.

"Can I speak to Mitch, please?"

The voice on the other end instantly sharpened. "Who is this, and what do you want with my fiancé?"

Katie stifled a laugh and put on her best sexy, innocent voice. "Oh...I think I have the wrong number."

"Don't play dumb with me," the woman snapped. "How do you know Mitch? Did he give you this number? Are you one of those girls from the bar?"

Lisa was wheezing silently into the pillow now, tears streaming down her cheeks.

Katie covered the mouthpiece, cackling, then took a deep breath, keeping the performance going. "Look, I don't want any trouble. Just tell Mitch—"

"Oh, I will tell Mitch," the woman growled.

Katie's eyes went wide. She slammed the phone down and burst into laughter. "Oh my god! She thinks Mitch is cheating with some girl from a bar!"

Lisa rolled onto her back, gasping for air. "We are going straight to hell."

"Only if she finds us first," Katie said, wiping her eyes.

Lisa reached for the phone, still giggling. "Your turn's over, prank master. Time for me to ruin someone's night."

"Look at you," Katie grinned. "Growing confidence and tapping into your naughty side. I'm so proud."

Lisa dialed a random number, her foot jittering nervously as the line rang. It went to voicemail, and she quickly hung up.

"Coward!" Katie teased.

"Shut up!" Lisa shot back, dialing again. This time, someone answered.

"Hello?"

Lisa took a deep breath, then whispered into the receiver, *"We know your secret."*

Katie lowered her voice to a whisper, adding the slightest rasp as she leaned into the receiver and whispered the same line. *"We know your secret."*

A pause. Then, a confused, half-asleep mumble. "Huh?"

Katie let the silence stretch just a little too long before repeating, slower this time. "We know what you did."

The line went dead.

Lisa burst into laughter, clutching her stomach. "Oh my god! That was so creepy."

Katie shrugged, grinning as she handed her the phone. "Go again and don't screw it up."

Lisa picked a random number and dialed. The person on the other end inhaled sharply. "This better be fucking important!"

Lisa slammed the phone down, her heart hammering.

Katie doubled over, tears in her eyes. "Holy shit! They were pissed!"

Lisa laughed, wiping her palms on her pajama pants. "This is feeling weird."

"Weirdly awesome," Katie corrected.

They went back and forth, making more calls, their whispers dripping through the receiver.

We know your secret.

We saw what you did.

You can't hide forever.

Most people just hung up, some cursed them out. Many didn't answer.

"One more call," Lisa said, "and then we really call it a night. Prank calling is exhausting."

"Fine," Katie nodded, remembering Tyler was supposed to come by. At least, she hoped he planned to.

"May I?" Lisa asked and Katie nodded.

Lisa dialed a number from memory, so nervous and eager, she forgot to hit *67 first and didn't even notice. The line rang.

Once.

Twice.

Click.

No hello. Just breathing, slow, steady, and too close, like the mouthpiece was resting against someone's lips.

Lisa's pulse skipped. "Uh... hello?"

"Yeah?" a man whispered. The voice was wrong somehow, too calm, too near, like he was already in the room.

Lisa glanced at Katie, suddenly uneasy. But she pushed through, trying to sound braver than she felt. She dropped her voice half an octave, flattening her tone to make it sound older, more detached.

"We know your secret," she whispered seductively.

A long, brittle silence. Then:

"What?"

Lisa hesitated, throat tightening. "...We saw what you did."

The breathing stopped.

"What do you think you saw?" the man asked, his voice flat now.

Katie sat up slowly, as she noticed the color draining from Lisa's face. She mouthed, *What's happening?*

Lisa tried to swallow but couldn't. "Wh—what?" Katie leaned into the phone to listen.

"I said," the man repeated, quieter this time, "what do you think you saw?"

Something shifted in the background. A creak. The sound of a door closing.

"Tell me," he said. "Tell me who this is and where you are."

Lisa slammed down the phone. For a second, all she could hear was the blood rushing in her ears.

For a moment, neither of them spoke. Lisa stared at the cordless phone, her fingers trembling slightly as she set it back on the receiver. The echo of that voice—"What do you think you know?"—lingered in the air like cigarette smoke.

Katie let out a breathy laugh. "Okay, that was way too real. Your delivery was spot on, but that guy? That guy sounded like he'd kill someone."

Lisa offered a weak smile but said nothing.

Katie stretched out on the floor again, the Cosmo quiz discarded by her side. "We should totally tell Tyler about that call. He'll lose his shit."

Lisa didn't respond. Her gaze had drifted to the front window. The curtains were closed, but she suddenly had the uncomfortable sensation of being watched. A ripple of unease stirred in her stomach.

Katie noticed. "You okay?"

"Yeah," Lisa said too quickly. "Just tired. Is Tyler coming soon?"

"No. Girls only, remember?"

Lisa hesitated. "Look, it's okay if he stops by. You don't have to feel bad just because I'm not dating any-one."

"I don't," Katie said, a little sharper than she meant to.

"Okay," Lisa mumbled.

A pause.

"That call freaked you out, huh?" Katie asked, watching her.

"Yeah," Lisa admitted, her voice quieter now. "A little. I need to tell you something—"

A sharp rattle cut her off.

Both girls froze.

It came from the front door. Soft at first, like someone testing the knob.

Then it shook again. Harder this time.

"What is that?" Katie whispered.

"I think it's the front door," Lisa replied, barely audible.

The rattling continued, then—

Ding-dong.

Katie's mouth opened, but no sound came out. Lisa's heart pounded so loudly she was sure Katie could hear it.

Another pause.

Ding-dong. Again.

Katie forced a nervous laugh. "We're scaring ourselves for no reason. It's probably just Tyler."

"So you did invite him?" Lisa asked.

"Yeah," Katie admitted. "I'm sorry I lied."

"Whatever," was all Lisa could think to reply.

They both stared at the front door. Katie suddenly realized she'd forgotten to turn on the porch light like she'd promised.

A shadow moved past the window.

Both girls screamed.

Then—silence.

Just the creaking of the swing outside.

Katie moved first, crawling over to the edge of the window as another sound came from outside, her breath shallow. She reached for the curtain, but stopped short.

"What are you doing?" Lisa hissed.

"I'm making sure it's Tyler so we can let him in," Katie said.

"No. Don't."

"What? Why?"

"What if it's not him?" Lisa asked, genuinely scared.

"Of course it's him," Katie said. "Who else would it be?"

Katie's fingers pulled the curtain back just an inch.

Nothing. No figure. No footsteps. Just the porch bathed in shadows, the swing creaking gently as it rocked itself.

Lisa stood, arms wrapped tightly around her body. "If it was Tyler, he would've said something."

Katie let the curtain fall shut again. "Maybe he thinks he's being funny. Playing a prank."

Neither of them moved.

Lisa's throat tightened. She felt like the walls were closing in.

"So why aren't you answering the door?" Lisa asked, her voice small.

Katie didn't respond. Her eyes were still locked on the window, as if something might press against it at any moment.

Then—

A single knock.

Soft.

Deliberate.

They both jumped.

Lisa backed toward the kitchen. "We should call the police."

"I think we're overreacting," Katie said, though even she didn't sound convinced.

Another knock.

Harder.

Closer.

This time, neither of them spoke.

And from the other side of the door, a voice shouted:

"Open the fucking door. I know you're in there."

CHAPTER 13

The phone started ringing as soon as Eric rushed into his apartment. He glanced at the clock. *12:57am.*

Who would be calling this late?

He kicked the door shut behind him and stood there for a second, catching his breath.

The apartment was freezing, the radiator long dead and a constant draft leaking through the cracked window by the sink. A single bare bulb buzzed overhead, casting everything in a dull yellow haze. The carpet was worn through in patches, and the walls still carried faint outlines of where past tenants hung photos.

It was all he could afford after Laura kicked him out.

One bedroom, no parking, water-stained ceiling, and a landlord who never answered the phone.

When Ellie came to visit, she tried to pretend it didn't bother her. She smiled, sat cross-legged on the lumpy couch, and talked about school like nothing was different. But he saw the way her eyes lingered on the peeling paint, the broken cabinet door, the dishes stacked in the sink. She never stayed long.

Eric ran a hand through his hair, jaw tightening.

He didn't plan to sit down, but he did, on the edge of the couch, jacket still on, blood stiff in the creases of his sleeves. The cigarette burned between his fingers, forgotten. The taste of iron still lingered in his mouth, metallic and strange, like biting a battery.

The phone rang again.

Once.

Twice.

His head snapped up. He didn't move at first. Just listened.

Click.

He answered without thinking. Didn't say hello. Just brought the receiver to his lips and breathed.

Slow.

Methodical.

Measured.

"Yeah?" he whispered.

He knew his voice was wrong. Too still. Too steady. But he didn't care.

A pause. Then a girl's voice—young, but trying to sound older, and nervous. "We know your secret."

Eric's blood turned colder than it already was.

He didn't speak. Just let the silence stretch.

Another beat. Then, quieter: "...We saw what you did."

He stopped breathing.

He sat straighter.

Everything in him locked into place.

There was something about the voice—something *off*. It scratched at the edge of memory. Familiar, but warped. Like hearing a song you used to know played underwater.

"What do you think you saw?" he said, his voice flat now.

He could hear someone in the background—another girl maybe. Movement and whispered panic.

The first girl spoke again, her voice pinched and dry. "Wh—what?"

"I said..." He stood slowly, the phone cord stretching as he moved. "...what do you think you saw?"

The apartment was silent except for the buzz of the overhead bulb. Eric found himself drifting toward the window, the phone still pressed to his ear. He pushed the curtain aside and peered into the darkness. Nothing but shadows and an empty street.

"Tell me," he said into the phone, colder now. "Tell me who this is and where you are."

Click.

They hung up.

He stayed there, holding the dead receiver to his ear for another ten seconds. Listening. Waiting.

Then, slowly, he smiled.

CHAPTER 14

K atie and Lisa stood frozen, eyes locked on the door.

Lisa felt the room shrink, every sound amplified—the tick of the wall clock, the low hum of the TV, the sound of their own shallow breathing.

Tap. Tap.

The sound came again. Not the doorbell this time. A knock. But not a normal knock—slow and spaced out, like whoever was on the other side was in no rush.

Each tap seemed to echo through the room, as if someone were testing the thinness of the barrier between them.

Lisa edged toward the window, her breath held tight in her chest. She reached for the curtain but hesitated.

Katie whispered, "Don't."

Lisa ignored her and pulled back the edge just enough to peek.

Nothing.

No one on the porch.

She let the curtain fall. "No one's there."

Katie looked like she might cry. "But someone rang. *Twice*. And knocked."

Lisa nodded slowly, her mind racing. "Maybe they're messing with us. Like, hiding in the bushes or something."

The phone on the couch lit up.

Neither girl moved.

Then another knock. Louder this time.

Thump thump thump.

A low voice outside whispered something neither of them could catch. The sound of words with no meaning, almost like a chant.

"Okay," Lisa whispered, "I'm calling 9-1-1." She ran to the phone and grabbed the receiver.

The doorknob jiggled. Katie screamed. Lisa yelped and dropped the phone.

A shadow shifted across the crack under the door. Something heavy shuffled on the porch, the boards creaking under its weight.

"Screw this," Katie said, grabbing a nearby lamp like a weapon.

Lisa hesitated only a second before lunging for the doorknob and yanking the door open.

A figure stood on the porch—and Katie didn't wait. She swung the lamp with everything she had.

"Whoa, *Jesus*!" the figure shouted, stumbling back just in time. The lamp whooshed past his head and slammed into the doorframe with a loud crack.

"Katie! What the hell? It's me!"

Both girls froze again, blinking.

"...Tyler!" Katie called in relief.

He stood there, hair tousled from the wind, cheeks pink with cold, breath puffing white into the night air, holding up a brown paper bag with a smug grin. He blinked at the two pale, wide-eyed girls staring back at him.

"Yeah! You guys okay? I've been outside for like five minutes."

Lisa slumped against the wall, exhaling hard. Katie groaned and dropped the broken lamp onto the couch. "You absolute idiot. We thought we were about to die!"

Tyler laughed and stepped inside, kicking the door shut behind him. He hung his keys on the hook near the entryway, like he always did at home, before holding up the bag.

"Well, sounds like you can definitely use this then," he said, pulling out a 40 like it was some kind of prize.

CHAPTER 15

Eric sat at his kitchen table, the faint glow of the clock on the microwave the only light in the room. He stared at the cordless phone on the table, replaying the call in his head.

"We know what you did."

His hands shook as he lit another cigarette, the flame briefly illuminating the deep lines etched into his face. He dragged in a lungful of smoke and exhaled slowly, watching the tendrils curl and dissipate in the dim light.

The phrase kept circling back, a relentless loop he couldn't escape. He'd been careful. But what if someone had actually seen something?

He tapped the ash off the cigarette, his mind racing. Maybe it was a bluff, some punk kid playing games. But the voice…it was familiar. Someone he knew.

Eric glanced at the clock again. Fifteen minutes had passed since the call, but the words still clawed at his brain. He stubbed out the cigarette in the ashtray, the filter joining a pile of half-smoked butts.

He shoved back the chair, its legs scraping the floor, and paced the length of the kitchen. His boots thudded heavily against the linoleum, the sound grating against his nerves.

There had to be a way to figure out who called him. He grabbed the phone and scrolled through the caller ID, a mix of familiar numbers and cryptic names he didn't recognize. His thumb stopped when he saw the most recent entry: M. Turner.

"Turner," he muttered under his breath, rolling the name around in his head. He had encountered many Turners over the years, but none that stuck except one. But it couldn't be. The name echoed like something half-remembered from a dream, familiar but blurred, as though glimpsed through a rain-streaked window. Still, something about the voice itched beneath his skin.

How did he know that voice?

He stood there a moment longer, the hum of the fridge filling the silence like static in his ears.

It wasn't just a prank. He knew the difference.

This wasn't some kid calling at random. Whoever it was...they knew something. Or *thought* they did. And that made them dangerous.

His eyes flicked toward the kitchen counter. Somewhere—he *knew*—he had a phone book. He checked the kitchen drawers first. Utensils. Coupons. Takeout Menus. Old batteries. No book. He moved to the living room. Opened the cabinet under the coffee table. Nothing but old TV guides and an ashtray full of loose change.

His search became more frantic. He dropped to his knees and looked under the couch, yanking aside a crumpled magazine and a balled-up sock. Still nothing.

"Come on," he growled. "I know you're here."

He stood, rubbing a hand through his hair, pacing now. Then his eyes landed on the hallway closet.

He yanked it open. A cascade of coats and tangled umbrellas spilled out. And there—jammed between a rolled-up welcome mat and a cracked shoebox—was the phone book.

He snatched it up and slammed it down on the dining table. The cover was bent, pages yellowed and curled, but it would do.

He flipped it open, scanning frantically. T... T... Turner...

Too many.

B. Turner. C. Turner. D & S Turner.

Nothing that leapt out.

He turned the page. Slower now. His eyes moved line by line until—

Turner, M. Just four names.

He pulled a pen from his jacket pocket and jotted the addresses onto a crumpled receipt.

M. Turner. Whoever she was—whoever had called him—was about to learn the difference between games and consequences.

Eric grabbed his Motorola Elite flip phone from the kitchen counter, the antenna already half-extended. He tucked it into his jacket pocket, the weight of it grounding him.

Then he shrugged on his coat and walked out.

The porch groaned beneath his boots. The air outside was colder than it should've been for that time of night. The wind bit at his cheeks and tangled his thoughts.

He locked the door behind him this time. If the girl on the phone wanted to play games, he'd play.

But first, he needed to find out exactly who *M. Turner* was.

And why her voice wouldn't leave his head.

Chapter 16

The living room smelled of popcorn and nail polish, the air tinged with acetone and warm butter.

Katie lay upside down on the couch, her feet draped over the back cushions, as Tyler opened the bottle of Olde English and took a sip.

"We're so going to regret this tomorrow," Lisa said.

Tyler passed the bottle to Katie. She sat up, took a long sip, and grinned. "It's already tomorrow."

Next, Lisa took a swig and made a face. "Gross," she muttered.

Tyler flopped down onto the floor, stretching out on the carpet. His eyes landed on the half-open pizza box beside the coffee table.

"Wait, you have pizza left?" He leaned over and opened the lid. "Hell yes. I'm starving."

"There were three left," Lisa said dryly. "But Katie ate one and tried to blame it on me."

Katie grinned, unapologetic. "You looked like you wanted it."

Tyler grabbed a slice and took a giant bite. "So what'd I miss?"

Katie leaned back against the couch, her voice light. "Not much. We cried over Skeet Ulrich, painted our nails, took some Cosmo quizzes, scared a few strangers with prank calls." She laughed but the back of her neck prickled as the wind rattled the windows.

"Wait, *actual* prank calls?"

Katie nodded proudly. "Those bastards didn't know what hit 'em."

Tyler shook his head, chewing. "You two are nightmares when you're together."

Outside, the wind picked up again. The porch swing let out a groan as it swayed slowly back and forth.

Lisa glanced toward the window, then back at her friends. For now, with Tyler here and the malt liquor making everything feel fuzzy around the edges, the weird phone call felt like something that had happened to someone else. She curled deeper into the couch cushions and let herself get lost in Katie's summary of the prank calls.

But even as she laughed, part of her stayed alert, afraid that the man she called would somehow find out who they are.

CHAPTER 17

Eric pulled up to the first address, a small ranch house with overgrown hedges and a mailbox that leaned at an awkward angle. The windows were dark except for a single porch light that flickered weakly against the night.

He sat in his car for ten minutes, waiting for any sign of life. But the house remained still. Then, finally, the lights turned on and through the window, Eric watched an elderly man shuffle past in a bathrobe. A moment later, an elderly woman appeared behind him, adjusting her housecoat and following him toward what looked like the kitchen.

Wrong house.

He pulled away from the curb and drove to the next address on his list.

The car's engine purred low as Eric parked halfway down the street. He killed the headlights but left the engine running, the dashboard casting his face in a dull green glow.

The house that sat just ahead was a two-story colonial with a porch that looked like it hadn't seen fresh paint in years. The porch light was off, but the living room window pulsed with shifting colors, the flicker of a television casting shadows that danced along the driveway.

Eric leaned forward, elbows on the wheel. Three figures inside. Teenagers. Two girls and a boy.

The taller girl had long, dark hair. The other had a streak of purple running through hers, and she moved like she was used to being the loudest voice in the room. The boy sat close to them—too close. His arm brushed the dark-haired girl's.

Eric's jaw flexed. His fingers tapped out a rhythm against the steering wheel that didn't match the beat of his heart.

His stomach dropped as he realized why the name on the caller ID was familiar. Why he had heard that voice before. For a moment, he couldn't breathe. The pieces slid together, forming a picture he didn't want to see. These weren't strangers taunting him. They knew him. Maybe they'd followed him after school, watching when he thought he was alone.

The how didn't matter anymore. What mattered was the certainty tightening around his chest: they knew what he'd done. And they had to be stopped.

He reached over to the passenger seat and picked up the baseball cap he always kept there. He pulled on the cap, tugging the brim low. He stared at the house through the windshield, watching the way the trio moved—relaxed, unguarded. Like they didn't know the world was full of consequences.

A burst of laughter broke through the night, high, sharp, and careless. It cut through him like glass.

He opened the door slowly and stepped out, leaving the engine running. The night swallowed him instantly.

The gravel beneath his boots gave a soft crunch as he moved toward the edge of the house. He froze. Waited.

Nothing stirred.

He watched through the window as the boy leaned back on his elbows, laughing at something. One of the girls tilted her head back, her lips parted in a smile.

Eric stepped off the curb and onto the damp grass, careful to avoid the sidewalk. One slip, one noise, and everything would be over. He moved like a shadow, staying low, circling wide to avoid the porch light's reach.

He paused beneath a tree just across from the living room window, watching.

They were passing around a bottle. Malt liquor, probably. Cheap. Illicit.

You think this is funny? he thought, his lip curling. *You think this is a game?*

His heart pounded, not from fear, but from something darker.

One wrong move and he could ruin everything. He needed to wait. Let them get comfortable. Let them forget the voice on the other end of the phone.

His boot slipped slightly on the slick grass. He tensed.

No reaction from inside.

Tyler got up, disappeared into the kitchen. The girls stayed put, still laughing. Still safe. For now.

Eric backed up, pressing himself into the shadows. He'd wait.

He could be patient.

He'd waited before.

CHAPTER 18

Evelyn Winslow couldn't sleep.

She hadn't slept well in years, not since her husband passed. She stood at her living room window, her fingers lightly brushing the edge of the lace curtain. In her other hand, she held a delicate porcelain teacup, the steam curling upward, warming her face.

The house was quiet except for the steady ticking of the grandfather clock in the hallway and the low hum of the refrigerator. The tea was chamomile, her usual for nights like this, when sleep wouldn't come no matter how many chapters she read or how long she stared at the ceiling.

From her perch on the hill, she had a clear view of the neighborhood. Her home sat a little higher than the rest, separated from her neighbors by carefully trimmed hedges and winding stretches of lawn dotted with garden statues her husband had chosen years ago.

The streetlights lining the road were spaced too far apart, leaving deep wells of shadow between amber pools of light. The way darkness could stretch its fingers so easily through their quiet little neighborhood always bothered her.

Her eyes drifted to the Turner house, about fifty yards down the street. The porch light was on, and faint flickers of a television glowed through the front windows. She squinted.

There was an unfamiliar car parked in the driveway. Small. Dark. Not the mother's, and certainly not that new husband's of hers.

Evelyn narrowed her eyes. The curtains weren't fully drawn. Through the sheer material, she could just make out three figures inside, two girls and a boy. They were huddled together on the floor surrounded by blankets and junk food. One of the girls lifted a bottle, tilting it back in a way Evelyn knew wasn't how you drank soda.

"Hmph. Boyfriends and drinking now too?" she muttered under her breath. "Teenagers these days."

They started laughing about something.

Evelyn sighed. Her daughter used to laugh like that.

But now, both her children lived states away, grown and busy, with families of their own. They called on holidays. Sent cards, sometimes. Promised to visit but rarely did. The last time her son came through town, he only stayed an hour.

So now it was just her. And Buster.

He was all she had left, really. The only one still tethered to her daily life. She talked to him more than she cared to admit. He listened better than most people she knew.

She let the curtain fall back into place and shook her head, but she didn't step away.

That's when she saw him.

A man, standing across the street near the hedge line, half-shadowed by the trees. Not walking. Not moving. Just standing there, staring toward the Turner house.

Her breath caught in her throat. There was something unnatural about how still he was, like he wasn't out for a stroll or waiting for anyone. He was watching.

Behind her, a low growl rumbled. Evelyn turned. Buster had padded silently into the room, his ears perked, eyes fixed on the window. His shaggy body was tense, tail stiff, head tilted.

"What is it, love?" she asked gently.

Buster let out a short, sharp bark, then trotted toward the front door.

Evelyn frowned. He never barked unless he meant it. Not at shadows. Not at passing cars.

She set her teacup down with a soft clink and stepped into the hallway, the familiar creak of the floorboard beneath her slippers grounding her for just a second.

Buster continued to growl. That man was still there. Lurking.

Evelyn's hand hovered over the rotary phone on the hall table, ready to call the police.

What would she even say?

A man is standing outside the Turner house?

They'd tell her she was imagining things again. Just like they had when she'd called about the prowler last fall, who turned out to be a UPS driver. Or the time she swore someone had been in her backyard but it was just a raccoon.

But Buster was still growling. And the man was still there.

She'd deal with this on her own.

CHAPTER 19

In the kitchen, Tyler rummaged through the refrigerator with one hand and held the beer with his other. The shelves were mostly bare except for half-empty condiments and a lonely carton of eggs.

He leaned back, holding the door open with his shoulder. "Lisa!" he called. "Does your mom ever buy food?"

From the living room came a chorus of laughter, Katie's louder than Lisa's.

Tyler was about to give up when he spotted a Tupperware container tucked behind the milk. He pulled it out, cracked the lid, sniffed. Pasta. Still smelled decent. Good enough for a drunken midnight snack.

He shut the fridge with his hip and padded toward the counter. The overhead light flickered once, buzzing faintly.

He glanced up. "The fuck?" he muttered, smirking.

But the smirk faded as he passed the sink and caught a glimpse of the backyard through the kitchen window.

The porch light cast a soft glow over the lawn and the tire swing, swaying lazily even though the air was now perfectly still.

He paused.

There was nothing *wrong* exactly, but something felt off. He couldn't put his finger on it, but he didn't like it.

He took a slow sip of beer, his eyes scanning the yard.

At first, he didn't see anything. Then, movement. Subtle. Just beyond the tree line at the edge of the yard.

Tyler blinked and leaned closer, trying not to fog the glass.

Nothing. Just shadows.

A faint rustle came from the tree line, barely audible but enough to raise the hairs on his neck.

He stepped back, brow furrowing.

"Hey," he called out casually, forcing a laugh into his voice, "either one of you invite some weirdo to crash the sleepover?"

Lisa responded with a snort. "If you mean you, then yes, but I wasn't the one to do it."

Katie didn't say anything.

Tyler hesitated, still staring out at the yard. He set the beer down and reached for the back door's deadbolt. It was unlocked.

He clicked it into place.

Then turned out the kitchen light.

"How about we turn on some music?" he said, grabbing the beer again and walking back into the living room.

CHAPTER 20

Evelyn slipped on her walking shoes, clipped the leash to Buster's collar, and grabbed her flashlight. The dog tugged her down the front steps and paused at the edge of the walkway, nose twitching. He stepped forward, alert, pulling slightly on the leash. Evelyn followed, her slippers whispering against the stone path.

He growled once, then again, this time louder, deeper.

Evelyn followed his gaze.

That's when she saw him again.

The figure.

Moving slowly, not far from the Turner house.

She froze. Buster stilled beside her, letting out a low, rumbling growl.

Whoever it was wasn't walking a dog. Wasn't out for a stroll. Wasn't doing anything that made sense at this hour.

And now, he wasn't moving at all.

He stood frozen, staring straight at the Turner house.

Evelyn's stomach tightened as the figure suddenly began moving toward it.

Buster barked again, louder this time, and the man hesitated—just for a second—before continuing.

Evelyn's grip on the leash clenched. She edged back toward the steps.

Something was wrong.

Very, very wrong.

"Excuse me!" Evelyn called out as she approached the man, her voice firm but wavering slightly. Her flashlight caught the figure mid-stride, illuminating the edges of his face for the first time. He stopped abruptly, turning toward her.

The man's face was partially obscured by the shadow of his baseball cap, but his jaw was tight, his posture tense.

"What are you doing?" Evelyn asked, stopping several feet away. She wasn't about to get too close, not yet. "Do you live around here?"

The man didn't respond, his eyes darting between Evelyn and the Turner house.

Evelyn raised her flashlight higher, the beam shining directly into his chest. "Well? Are you going to answer me? Because I'll have you know this is a quiet neighborhood and I am part of the neighborhood watch. We don't tolerate troublemakers."

He finally spoke, his voice low and gravelly. "I'm not causing any trouble, ma'am."

"You're standing outside a house like a prowler," Evelyn shot back. "And I don't think the police will buy that excuse. I called them and they're on the way," she lied.

The man took a step toward her, and Evelyn instinctively stepped back.

"Listen, lady," he said, his voice sharpening. "I don't think this is any of your business."

Her heart quickened, but she stood her ground. "It is my business when someone's lurking where they don't belong."

"My daughter lives here," Eric said.

"What?" Evelyn demanded, just to be sure she'd heard him right.

"My daughter."

"Oh, you're the Turner girl's father."

"Yeah," Eric said, too quickly. Too carelessly.

Evelyn took a half-step back, the gravel crunching beneath her slippers. "So why are you standing out here? Why don't you go inside?"

Eric didn't answer right away. "Just out for some air."

"We met once," she said, narrowing her eyes. "When the girl was little. Wasn't your name Richard or Robert or something?" Her tone was almost casual, but her eyes didn't leave his face.

Eric didn't respond.

"And you—" she tilted her head, studying him in the moonlight, "—you don't look like the man I met back then. It was a long time ago but I never forget a face."

Eric's jaw tightened.

"The girl watches Buster sometimes. There's a picture with her father in the living room. I see it when I pick him up. But that's not you, is it?"

"That picture is from a long time ago," Eric muttered.

"Mm. Maybe." Evelyn didn't move. "So what's your daughter's name?"

Eric's hands flexed at his sides.

"You're awful quiet all of a sudden," she said, voice colder now. "You say you're her father, but you're standing out here in the dark, creeping around. That doesn't sit right with me."

Eric tilted his head, the look on his face hardening into something darker. "You shouldn't have come out here."

Evelyn blinked. "Excuse me?"

He took a slow step toward her.

"Don't come any closer," she said, shining the flashlight into his face, voice rising.

Before Evelyn could react, Eric lunged forward. The flashlight slipped from her grasp as he grabbed her wrist, yanking her toward him. She tried to scream, but his other hand clamped over her mouth, muffling the sound.

Buster exploded into barking, nails skittering against the concrete as he bounded toward them. The flashlight rolled across the driveway, casting jagged shadows as the dog leapt, teeth snapping at Eric's arm.

"Get off!" Eric snarled, jerking his elbow back. The dog bit down harder, growling deep in his throat, shaking with feral intensity.

Evelyn's slippers scraped against the concrete as she struggled, but Eric was too strong. With one swift motion, he kicked Buster aside and slammed her against the side of the garage.

Her head struck the metal with a sickening crack, and her legs buckled beneath her. She fell sideways onto the walkway, half turned toward the street, and slumped to the ground, her breath shallow and ragged.

Eric crouched over her, his shadow swallowing her frame. He stared at her for a long moment, breathing hard. "I warned you," he muttered, his voice dripping with quiet fury.

Buster whimpered, then barked again, circling, teeth bared, as Evelyn's vision blurred and the world around her faded into darkness.

CHAPTER 21

Eric crouched in the shadows behind the garage, chest heaving. He hadn't meant to kill her. But when she started asking all those questions, something in him surged, sudden and blinding. By the time he came back to himself, she was on the ground. He drew in a breath of cold air, trying to steady his nerves.

Inside the Turner house, music played, soft and cheerful. A pop song from the 80s. The kind Ellie used to sing in the back seat.

He looked toward the house. Then back at Evelyn. He couldn't leave her here.

Something rustled to his left. A twig snapped.

He turned sharply, ready to retreat, but it was just the dog. Its hackles were raised, a low growl in its throat.

Evelyn's robe was soaked through, the fabric darkened around her hairline and neck. Her hand twitched before falling still. Her eyes remained open, glazed and glassy.

Eric slipped deeper into the shadows behind the garage. The mutt barked once, sharp and high, then lunged a step forward, teeth flashing in the dim light. It stopped just short, snarling, as if it knew it couldn't stop him but refused to let him go without a fight.

Inside, the music got louder. Eric crouched beside the old woman's body. He glanced toward the house. No movement in the windows. The music had changed—something upbeat now.

He wrapped his fingers around Evelyn's wrist. Cold. Lighter than he expected. He pulled her gently at first, then faster, dragging her across the stone path and into the shadows of the hedges that lined her garden.

Leaves whispered as her body slipped into the undergrowth, one slipper falling off and bouncing once before landing sideways in the grass. Her hand, limp and pale, snagged on a rose bush. He pried it loose.

Behind him, the dog barked again, harsher this time, the sound echoing off the garage. When Eric turned,

Buster stood at the edge of the porch, ears flattened, hackles bristling, a growl rattling deep in his chest.

Eric turned slowly. Buster stood frozen at the edge of the porch, ears flattened, a low rumble shaking his chest.

"Go on," Eric said softly, eyes meeting the dog's. "You don't want this."

Buster didn't move.

Eric ducked back into the shadows and dragged a broken section of wooden paneling over the body. Not perfect, but enough for now.

From inside, a burst of laughter. A girl's voice.

He glanced up. The living room glowed warm through the curtains.

Eric backed away from the hedge, disappearing behind the side of the house. He paused once more to look at the dog.

Buster wasn't barking. Good.

Time to move.

Chapter 22

The living room glowed in dim golden light, string lights draped lazily across the ceiling. The stereo played low in the background—"Name" by Goo Goo Dolls—its opening chords soft and sorrowful, bleeding gently into the room.

And even though the moment passed me by / I still can't turn away...

Katie stretched her legs across Tyler's lap, giggling as he tried to balance the half-warm bottle of malt liquor on her shin. Lisa, sitting cross-legged beside them, hummed along absentmindedly, her gaze distant, unfocused.

Then—

BARK. BARK. BARK.

All three of them froze.

"That sounds close," Tyler said, sitting up.

Another bark, sharper this time, edged with something urgent. Then a low, guttural growl.

Lisa frowned. "Who lets their dog out this late?"

Katie rose and padded to the window, pushing the curtain aside. "I don't see anything. It's too dark."

"I'll check it out," Tyler said.

"Want company?" Katie asked.

"Nah, I'll be two seconds. Probably just some stray."

He stepped out into the cool night, the music behind him dimming as the door swung shut.

The porch light buzzed above him, casting a soft halo across the lawn.

"Here, boy," Tyler muttered. "Or girl. Or demon. Let's find out."

From behind a low hedge, a shape crept forward, cautious and silent. A dog. Small, shaggy, visibly shaking.

Tyler blinked. "Hey there."

The dog stopped at the bottom of the steps, tail low, eyes wide.

Tyler crouched, keeping his voice low. "You lost?"

The dog sniffed his hand once, then slowly stepped forward. Tyler clipped his fingers gently around its collar.

"No tag," he muttered. "Where the hell did you come from?"

He stood and opened the front door again.

Lisa looked up as the dog padded inside, nails clicking against the hardwood.

And froze.

"Oh my god."

Katie turned. "What?"

Lisa dropped to her knees, hands hovering near the dog's face.

"That's Buster."

Tyler frowned. "What, like your dog?"

Lisa shook her head. "No. Evelyn's. My neighbor. He never leaves her side. Even when I dogsit sometimes, he just cries for her."

Katie's eyes widened. "You think she let him out?"

"No," Lisa said. "She wouldn't do that. He must have gotten out on his own."

They stared at the dog, who now sat trembling near the door, his eyes locked on something none of them could see.

The music played on in the background.

I saw the world spin beneath you / And scatter like ice from the spoon...

Buster whined, pressing closer to Lisa's side.

"I should take him home," she said, rising slowly. "He looks scared."

"Hold up," Tyler said. "Let me come with you."

Lisa shook her head. "I'll be fine. She's just across the street."

Katie stepped forward. "Fine, but I'm staying on the porch to watch."

Lisa gave a tight nod and reached for Buster's leash trailing behind him, then opened the door. Cool night air drifted in. The house seemed to exhale.

Lisa looked back at them. "I'll knock. If she's fine, I'll come right back."

Katie watched as her best friend and the dog disappeared down the porch steps into the dark.

The stereo hummed softly in the background.

...and now you're gone, it's like an echo in my mind...

Katie stepped onto the porch and crossed her arms, scanning the street.

The world outside felt different now—emptier.

Like something was watching. Waiting.

Lisa's figure moved steadily toward the Winslow house, Buster trotting beside her, the leash dragging slightly through the grass.

"Come on, buddy," she whispered. "Almost home."

But Buster stopped just before the walkway. His body stiffened, head low, ears flat.

Then he turned and faced the hedge.

A deep growl rumbled in his chest.

Lisa tugged gently on the leash. "Hey—no. Come on, it's okay."

Buster didn't move. He barked once, sharp and sudden, toward the base of the bushes.

Lisa flinched, her eyes flicking toward the shadowy hedge.

She squinted her eyes but saw nothing.

Probably a cat. Or a squirrel. Or some random nocturnal creature.

Still, she couldn't shake the feeling that something *was* there.

Her voice lowered. "It's just the wind, boy. Let's go."

She knelt beside him, ran a soothing hand down his back. He was trembling.

Katie, still watching from the porch, took a cautious step forward. "Everything okay?"

Lisa looked back and gave a small nod. "He's just spooked. Probably a raccoon."

She stood again, urging Buster toward Evelyn's door. He followed, hesitant, tail still tucked.

The bush behind them remained still.

But in its deepest shadow, Evelyn gave her final breath.

CHAPTER 23

Eric moved silently along the side of the house, his breath shallow, the cold air tightening in his lungs. The porch light spilled weakly across the lawn, but beyond that, the shadows were thick, broken only by the occasional flicker of streetlight or the dull blue glow from a neighbor's TV upstairs.

He crouched behind a hedge, just out of sight. From there, he could still see the front of the house. The door opened again.

A figure stepped out.

It was Lisa. She had the dog with her.

Eric narrowed his eyes, straining to see more, but she stayed mostly in silhouette, her dark hair pulled back, shoulders hunched slightly from the cold.

She said something to Katie still standing on the porch, then descended the steps, the leash trailing in her hand.

Eric tilted his head, watching her walk. Something about her gait. Confident, but cautious.

He stayed low, tracking her path as she made her way across the street.

She paused at the base of the Evelyn's porch. Lifted her hand and knocked.

Eric stayed in the shadows, unmoving. When Lisa was sure Evelyn wouldn't answer, she headed back across the street with the dog in tow.

Eric's eyes followed her until she was gone from view.

Only then did he rise from the hedge, the cold air filling his lungs like ice.

CHAPTER 24

L isa reached the edge of Evelyn's walkway, Buster still bristling at her side. The wind had picked up, rustling through the hedges that lined the yard like a warning whispered too softly to understand.

The bushes were thick here, dense with tangled branches and creeping ivy, left to grow wild beneath Evelyn's careful facade of a tidy home.

Buster gave another low growl and barked again, straining slightly toward the hedge.

"Shh," Lisa whispered, giving the leash a gentle tug. "It's nothing, Buster. It's okay."

But she didn't believe it.

She couldn't see anything in the dark, but the shadows under those hedges looked too deep, like they were swallowing the space beneath them.

Lisa swallowed hard. Her skin prickled.

She didn't want to be here anymore.

She stepped up onto the porch and tried the door. Locked. Of course.

She knocked, softer than she meant to. "Mrs. Winslow?"

No answer.

Buster whined.

Lisa knocked again, a little harder. "It's Lisa. We found Buster. Are you okay?"

Still nothing.

Her fingers hovered over the doorknob again, then pulled back. The windows were dark. No movement inside.

She rang the doorbell and waited.

"She's probably asleep," she told Buster. "Guess you're spending the night."

Lisa turned quickly and led him back across the street.

She never saw the figure hidden in the shadows, eyes following her every step.

Chapter 25

Lisa and Katie walked back into the house. Lisa shut the door behind her, locking it with a soft click. The living room welcomed her with its cozy amber glow and the low hum of the stereo, still playing the same Goo Goo Dolls song, now nearly at its end.

Buster trotted inside beside her, still jittery. His nails clicked on the hardwood, and he pressed close to her leg like a nervous child.

Katie pushed herself off the arm of the couch. "She okay?"

Lisa hesitated. "I don't know. I knocked and rang the bell. No answer."

Tyler raised an eyebrow. "She's probably just asleep."

"Yeah it's really late," Katie agreed. She glanced at Buster, who had now curled up beside the couch, his eyes trained on the front window. Every few seconds, he let out a soft whine.

Something about the sound made the room feel smaller.

Tyler tried to lighten the mood. "Maybe she had too much wine and passed out. My aunt used to do that. You could throw a marching band at her window and she wouldn't flinch."

Lisa didn't smile.

"She always leaves the porch light on. Every night. She watches the neighborhood like it's her job."

Katie crossed her arms. "Should we... call someone?"

Lisa bit her lip. "Like who? The police?"

Tyler flopped back onto the couch. "Because someone isn't answering their door in the middle of the night? They'd laugh us off the line. Let's wait. You can take the dog back in the morning."

Lisa hovered near the window, looking out. The wind had picked up again, swaying the tire swing on its rope. The creaking was faint, but persistent.

Katie glanced at the stereo. "Should we turn this off?"

"No," Lisa said quickly. "Leave it on."

The quiet in between songs felt heavier now.

Buster let out a low, rumbling growl.

All three turned.

He hadn't moved, just lifted his head. Still staring at the front window.

Katie moved closer to him. "You okay, buddy?"

He didn't blink.

Lisa backed away from the glass and pulled the curtains shut.

"We just lock up," she said softly. "Everything. All the doors. Windows too."

Tyler stood. "You sure we're not being a little—"

"I'm sure," Lisa cut in.

Katie nodded. "Yeah. Let's just lock up. And maybe stay together for the rest of the night. Can you stay, Tyler?"

"Yeah, sure. Not like my parents ever question where I am."

Outside, the porch swing groaned louder as the wind shifted again.

And not far from the window, just beyond the hedge, Eric watched the curtains fall shut, his breath steady, his eyes unblinking.

CHAPTER 26

Eric crouched behind the garage, letting the dark wrap around him like an old coat. He listened.

The house had gone quiet. The music, still playing, was barely audible from here, muffled by walls, thinned by distance. But he could still feel it, humming faintly in the soles of his feet.

He waited a few minutes longer. Long enough to let their nerves settle.

Then he moved.

Staying low, he crept around to the front of the house. The porch light had clicked off. The windows glowed faintly behind sheer curtains.

On the porch was a rusted plant stand, top-heavy with a cracked ceramic pot. Eric gripped the metal base and yanked, once, then again until the stand broke free. The bottom edge was jagged, bent where it had snapped from its frame.

He crouched in front of the door and drove the sharp end into the lock.

Thunk.

Snap.

Crack.

He twisted hard until something inside the deadbolt gave way with a metallic crunch. The bolt warped, grinding deep into the strike plate. Anyone trying to open the door from the inside later wouldn't be able to.

He let the plant stand fall with a hollow clang into the bushes.

Then he slipped away into the dark, circling toward the back of the house, where he saw a low, cracked concrete patio and a narrow side door, probably to the laundry room or kitchen. He tested the knob. Locked.

On the patio table sat an old flathead screwdriver, its handle faded from sun, like it had been waiting for him.

Eric smiled.

He picked it up, tested its weight, then jammed the tip into the seam between the door and frame.

One shove. Then another.

Pop.

A soft crack echoed into the night.

The door creaked open.

Inside, the air was thick and still.

Eric stepped over the threshold, careful not to let the door slam behind him.

The floor creaked beneath his boots. He paused.

Listened.

Silence.

They hadn't heard. Good.

He moved slowly through the laundry room, past a basket of clean clothes and a bottle of orange Tide. The hum of the refrigerator buzzed faintly from the next room.

He passed into the kitchen. Pale moonlight stretched across the tiled floor. A cereal bowl sat in the sink.

It was domestic. Lived-in. Normal.

It reminded him of the kitchen he once shared with his family. He could almost see Ellie at the table, feet swinging, hair tousled from sleep, excitedly telling Laura about a dream she'd had.

Eric blinked hard. Not now.

The hallway stretched out before him, dim and quiet. He could hear the soft pulse of music from the living room. Another song now, something slower.

He stayed close to the wall.

From the shadows, he watched their silhouettes—three teenagers and a dog—huddled in a triangle of light, moving in rhythm with the music.

They were laughing again.

It echoed in his head.

He thought of the phone call.

We know your secret.

Eric stepped back into the dark and disappeared behind the staircase.

He was inside now.

Time to scare them a bit.

Then find out exactly what they knew.

CHAPTER 27

Katie was the first to laugh again. It wasn't forced, but it was quieter than before. The kind of laugh people let out when they're trying to ignore a bad feeling.

Lisa had changed into pajama shorts and an oversized hoodie. Her minimal makeup was wiped clean. She'd tied her hair up in a messy bun and sat cross-legged on the floor, the edge of a blanket tucked beneath her.

Tyler had taken over the stereo, skipping through CDs until he landed on something familiar: Alanis Morissette's *Jagged Little Pill*.

"Hell yeah," Katie said, flopping back onto the couch. "Let the emotional spiral begin."

Tyler handed her the bottle. "Your turn to suffer through the last of the Olde E."

Katie took a swig and made a face. "Tastes like regret."

Lisa smiled faintly, but her eyes kept drifting to the window. She'd pulled the curtains shut earlier, but she still felt like something waited just beyond them.

Buster lay beside her, his head resting on his paws, eyes flicking toward the hallway every so often, as though waiting for someone to appear.

He hadn't stopped trembling.

Tyler noticed. "Is he always like that?"

Lisa shook her head. "No. He can get anxious but he seems scared. He's probably just confused being in a strange house."

"Or he senses a ghost," Katie added, waggling her fingers.

Lisa gave her a flat look. "Don't."

Another track started—*"You Oughta Know."* Katie began mouthing the lyrics dramatically, hairbrush in hand like a microphone.

For a few minutes, it felt peaceful.

The house breathed around them.

Until something shattered.

It came from upstairs, sharp and distinct.

Glass.

The music stopped.

All three froze.

Lisa turned toward the hallway. "Did you hear—"

Katie cut her off. "Yes."

Buster was already on his feet, ears up, tail stiff. He growled.

Tyler stood slowly. "Probably a picture frame. Maybe it fell off the wall?"

"I guess that's possible," Lisa said, her voice thin, dread curling in her chest.

They all looked toward the stairs.

The silence stretched.

Then came a creak from the second floor.

"That wasn't a picture frame," Katie said.

Tyler moved toward the stairs, but Lisa grabbed his arm. "Wait."

Another creak. Then footsteps.

"Someone's up there," Katie whispered.

Buster's growl deepened, the fur along his spine bristling. He padded toward the staircase, nose lifted, scenting the air.

Tyler gently pulled free from Lisa's grip. "Stay here with Katie. I'll check it out."

"Like hell," Lisa said. "We stick together."

The footsteps stopped directly above them. Then came the unmistakable sound of a door closing. Softly. Carefully.

Katie's face had gone pale. "There's no way that's just the house settling."

Tyler grabbed a poker from beside the fireplace. "Whoever's up there knows we're down here."

The three of them stood at the base of the stairs, looking up into the darkness of the second floor. Buster whined, torn between his protective instincts and some deeper fear.

"Should we call the police?" Lisa asked.

Before anyone could answer, they heard it again—another door, this time opening with a long, drawn-out creak.

And then, the sound of humming drifted down from upstairs.

A man's voice, soft and melodic, humming a familiar tune.

Katie's brow furrowed. She tilted her head, listening.

"Wait..." she whispered. "That's Alanis. *You Oughta Know*. We just listened to *it*."

Tyler looked up sharply. Lisa froze.

The humming continued, slow and deliberate, winding through the chorus like a lullaby.

You, you, you oughta know...

And in that moment, they knew for certain—

they weren't alone in the house.*

CHAPTER 28

The humming went on for what felt like an eternity, each note floating down through the floorboards like a ghost's whisper. Lisa found herself holding her breath, afraid that even the smallest sound might draw the stranger's attention to exactly where they stood.

Tyler's knuckles had gone white around the poker, and Katie had moved closer to the wall, as if she could somehow disappear into it. Then, as abruptly as it had begun, the humming stopped.

Lisa opened her mouth to say something, but the sound of the landline ringing stopped her.

They all held their breathe.

"Who the hell is calling this late?" Tyler finally asked.

Lisa moved first, walking toward the kitchen where the old cordless phone sat charging on its cradle. She picked it up slowly, holding it like it might burn her.

"Hello?"

Silence.

"Hello?"

Silence.

Then—

"I found you."

Lisa's breath caught.

"Who is this?" she whispered.

"You know," the voice whispered.

Click.

The line went dead.

Katie's voice cracked. "Who was it?"

Lisa swallowed. "I don't know." But deep down, she had a feeling. Only one person she'd called that night had sounded like that. The man she'd dialed on purpose.

"What did they say?"

"He said I found you."

Then everything went black.

The lights. The stereo. Even the little blinking green on the microwave.

Total darkness swallowed the house in an instant.

The girls screamed. Buster let out a single, sharp bark.

"What the hell—" Tyler said in surprise.

"Power outage?" Lisa offered, but even as she said it, her voice shook.

"That would be one hell of a coincidence," Katie whispered. "Let's get the fuck out of here."

"It'll be okay," Tyler said.

"We should have a flashlight in the kitchen." Lisa darted out of the room, her footsteps light but fast. She rummaged through the junk drawer full of receipts, pens, takeout menus. Finally, her fingers closed around cold metal. "Got it," she whispered, flicking the flashlight on.

She rushed back into the living room, the beam cutting a weak path across the floor, barely making a dent in the dark.

"Great. I'll check the fuse box," Tyler said.

"Okay," Lisa responded, handing him the flashlight.

The upstairs remained completely silent.

Then—

A soft knock.

From inside the house.

Katie backed toward the couch. "That wasn't the door."

Tyler stopped walking. Buster growled again, louder now. Somewhere in the house, a faint floorboard creaked. Lisa rushed in, shining the flashlight.

Tyler took a small step toward the hallway.

Lisa grabbed his arm. "Don't."

His jaw was tight. "Don't you want to know who's up there?"

"No, I'd rather live. Thanks," Katie said.

The flashlight flickered. Buster growled again.

And upstairs, Eric planned his next move.

CHAPTER 29

Eric moved carefully through the upstairs hallway, but his shoulder caught the edge of a picture frame hanging on the wall. It crashed to the floor, glass scattering across the hardwood.

He froze.

The music downstairs stopped.

After a moment, he crouched at the top of the stairs, listening to the rhythm of their hushed, worried voices below. Every sound scraped at his nerves.

Without meaning to, he began to hum. Soft, under his breath. The same song he'd just heard bleeding from their stereo—Alanis Morrisette, *You Oughta Know*. The melody curled out of him slow and low.

He reached into his coat pocket and pulled out the crumpled receipt. The number was still there, scrawled in pen that had bled slightly from sweat or rain. He couldn't remember which. *Had it been raining?*

He stopped humming.

Then he pulled out his Motorola Elite. The keypad glowed a dull green as he flipped it open and began to dial.

It wouldn't trace. He knew that. He'd bought the prepaid card in cash, not because he had something to hide, but because it was all he could afford. And because, deep down, he still needed a way to talk to Ellie.

The line rang once.

Then a familiar voice.

"Hello?"

He didn't speak at first. Just took a deep breath and let the quiet stretch.

"Hello?" she repeated.

Then, low and steady—

"I found you."

A beat of silence.

"Who is this?"

"You know who."

He hung up.

The click echoed louder in his ears than it should have.

He stared down at the green-lit screen for a moment, then powered the phone off and slid it back into his pocket.

He stood still, barely breathing, and let the silence settle around him.

Eric stepped into the guest room and opened the closet. The fuse box waited behind the coats, its metal face dull and scratched.

He hesitated.

A part of him—not rational, not hopeful, but human—whispered to stop.

He closed his eyes.

And saw Ellie.

Not how she was at the end. But before. Singing softly in the backseat. Talking about a boy in her class. Asking for Taco Bell on the way to school.

You can still walk away. They're just kids. Like she was. They don't know anything. Maybe it was a joke. A weird coincidence. No! He couldn't take that chance.

His hand trembled.

Then tightened.

He flipped the switch.

And the house went dark.

Chapter 30

The air shifted.

Lisa could feel it, heavy and close, like the whole house had sucked in a breath and refused to let it out.

Tyler's eyes were fixed on the hallway, his body rigid, as if bracing for something to lunge from the dark. The flashlight trembled in his grip, the fire poker in his other hand ready to strike.

Another sound, a floorboard groaning, slow and steady, from somewhere just out of sight.

Katie shook her head. "Hell no. Why aren't we running out the fucking front door?"

Buster's growl deepened. He took a single step forward, fur raised along his spine, his entire body humming with tension.

Tyler moved before anyone could stop him, reaching for the fireplace poker resting against the hearth.

Lisa shivered. "He said it. He said he found me." She started to cry.

Katie placed a hand on her shoulder. "If we get out of this house, we'll be fine."

Tyler moved before anyone could stop him, tightening his grip on the fire poker.

Buster stood guard near the hallway, ears up, body rigid. He growled again, low and steady.

Then—

Another sound from upstairs.

A creak.

Heavy.

Not pipes. Not settling.

A footstep.

Lisa shivered. "We need to call the police first."

"The cordless won't work if the power's out," Katie said.

"I have a car phone," Tyler offered.

"Yes," Katie muttered. "A fact I try to forget since this isn't the '80s and you don't work on Wall Street."

Tyler shot her a look. "Not the best time for jokes."

Before anyone could respond, Buster barked again, sharp and loud, facing the stairs.

Lisa jumped. Tyler took a step forward, but Lisa grabbed his arm. "We stay together. We move together."

Katie and Tyler nodded. "Front door," Tyler whispered. "Fast."

Lisa didn't argue. She moved first, the flashlight trembling slightly in her grip. The others followed close, Buster sticking to her like a shadow.

The entryway loomed ahead. The little side table with the bowl of keys, the framed photo of Lisa and her mom, the floral rug—they all looked different in the dark.

Lisa reached for the deadbolt.

It was already unlocked.

That stopped her cold.

"I... I locked this," she said quietly. "I locked it earlier."

Katie stepped beside her, deadpan. "Well, the person upstairs didn't crawl up the side of the house, Lisa."

Tyler moved past them and tried the handle. It didn't budge.

"What the fuck?"

He shoved harder. Nothing.

"It's stuck," he muttered. "No. It's jammed. From the outside."

Lisa backed away, heart hammering, trying to breathe. She turned to Tyler. "Garage. There's a side window. We break it, scream, run."

No one questioned it.

They bolted down the hallway, past the kitchen and into the attached garage. The air inside was colder, metallic. It smelled like gasoline and old tools.

Lisa found the hanging cord and yanked it hard. The garage door disconnected from the track with a loud clunk.

It groaned. Shifted.

Buster barked behind them, spinning in frantic circles.

"Lift—now!" Tyler growled.

All three of them lifted the door. Inch by inch, the garage door rose, groaning with the weight. Cold air spilled in. Moonlight. The open night.

Freedom.

"Go!" Lisa said.

Katie ducked down and rolled onto the driveway.

Tyler pushed from underneath, then slipped out after her.

As Lisa bent to follow, Buster froze.

"Come on!" she hissed, tugging at his leash. "Please—come on, come on, come on—"

He wouldn't move.

Behind her—

Footsteps.

A shadow.

The garage door slammed down with a crash.

Lisa screamed.

On the other side, Katie and Tyler pounded their fists against the door. "LISA!"

Inside, Lisa whirled around—

Eric stepped out from the shadows of the laundry room.

Calm. Focused.

The flashlight slipped from Lisa's hand and clattered to the floor.

She backed away, her breath catching. The garage was too dark.

The pounding on the garage door got louder, Katie and Tyler screaming Lisa's name.

"If it's really you," she whispered. "Please don't do this."

No answer.

But there was movement.

A shift in the shadows near the laundry room door.

The man stepped forward.

The shape solidified.

He stepped into the sliver of moonlight that leaked beneath the garage window.

Recognition struck like a match, confirming Lisa's fear.

"Ohmigod," Lisa couldn't hide her surprise. "It *is* you."

CHAPTER 31

Katie's fists slammed against the garage door again.

"LISA!" she screamed. "Are you okay?!"

Nothing.

Just Buster barking from the other side.

And then—

A man's voice. Calm. Close.

Katie stepped back, her breath caught in her throat. "Oh my god. Someone's in there with her."

Tyler's jaw clenched. "We have to get in there." He tried to lift the garage door again, with no luck.

"The front door," he said. "Let's try it again."

They took off around the side of the house, shoes slipping in the wet grass.

Katie was ahead when her foot caught on something—soft but solid—and she stumbled hard, catching herself on her palms.

"Shit—"

She looked down.

At first, it didn't register.

A robe. A leg. A pale hand curled near the hedge.

Then her brain caught up.

Katie screamed and stumbled back, bile rising in her throat.

"Tyler—Tyler, she's dead—"

"What?"

Katie pointed. She couldn't speak.

Tyler's face drained of color.

He pulled her up, gripping her arm tightly. "Come on. We're not wasting another second."

They raced up the porch steps. Katie's hand shook as she grabbed the knob. Still jammed.

Tyler dropped to one knee, flashlight scanning the doorframe. "There. Something's wedged under."

He shoved once. Nothing.

"Wait," Katie said, breathless. She darted to the porch railing, grabbed the broom leaning against it, and handed it to him.

Tyler wedged the handle under the door and pried hard.

A loud crack.

The door finally swung inward.

They stepped into the house.

The air inside was still. Heavy.

Too quiet.

They moved toward the garage door, slow and silent.

As they got closer, they heard a man's voice. Low. Calm. Muffled.

Followed by Lisa's. Shaky. Small.

"Why are you doing this?"

Tyler stopped in his tracks, eyes going wide. He turned to Katie.

"I'm going in," he said, already moving. "I'm going to get her."

He met her gaze.

"Go to the car. My keys are on the hook by the door. Call the police. Lock the doors. Don't wait for me."

Katie opened her mouth to argue, but he was already disappearing into the dark, toward the garage door.

CHAPTER 32

Eric stared at Lisa. He didn't flinch. Didn't speak.

"Please say something," Lisa pleaded.

His silence unnerved her. "Mr. Donner, why are you doing this?" she screamed.

His eyes narrowed. "Lisa. I didn't know it was you at first," he said finally, like he was convincing himself more than her. "Why did you call me? What do you know?"

She tried to swallow, but her throat felt like it was closing.

She could lie. Pretend it was random. A number in the phone book. A coincidence.

But it wasn't.

She'd known exactly who she was calling. She'd tried to tell Katie before Tyler showed up and derailed everything, scaring them both. But she didn't know what Mr. Donner was talking about—what secret he thought she'd uncovered.

All she knew was that she missed the sound of his voice on weekends. His calm, measured way of speaking. The way he said her name like it mattered. Like she did.

And for a short while, maybe she had.

It had only happened twice. After school. Once in his car, once in a hotel room. He'd said it couldn't happen again. That it had been a mistake. That he was going through a divorce and not thinking clearly. But she had been thinking clearly. She knew she wanted to be with him.

She found his new number. Memorized it. She wasn't proud of that, not now. But it had felt harmless then.

When she dialed that night, giggling with Katie on the couch, she knew who she was calling.

She just wanted to hear him.

To feel seen again.

But she couldn't say any of that out loud. Not now. Not to him.

Lisa's chest rose and fell, sharp and fast.

Buster pressed against her leg, trembling, growling low.

"It was just a joke," she said, the words tumbling out. "It was late and stupid and we were just messing around. I wanted to hear your voice. It's been so long since we were alone together."

"But you said you knew," Eric said, stepping closer. "You said it like you meant it." His voice cracked, wild around the edges.

He was unraveling right in front of her.

Lisa took a shaky step back. "I don't know anything. I swear."

A flicker of hesitation.

Then something darker took over.

"Don't fucking lie to me," Eric screamed.

"I'm not," Lisa cried out, her sobs breaking through. "I promise."

His hands grabbed her wrists. She twisted and kicked, slamming her heel into his shin.

Buster barked and launched forward, teeth flashing.

He jumped up and sank them into Eric's arm.

Eric roared, staggering. Lisa scrambled back, nearly free—

But Eric yanked Buster off and hurled him into the shelves. Tools clattered. The dog yelped and hit the floor, stunned.

Lisa turned back toward the door.

But he caught her.

They crashed into the concrete.

She fought—screamed—flailed with everything she had.

Her glasses flew off.

The flashlight skidded across the floor.

Lisa squinted up at him, breathing hard, face streaked with sweat and tears. Her lips parted, a quivering breath escaping as she tried to twist her head away.

But he lowered himself closer, trembling, lips brushing her damp hair, then pressing against her forehead. She flinched, a choked sound catching in her throat.

A desperate kiss followed, clumsy and confused, landing on her mouth. Her eyes went wide, panic flaring as she shoved weakly against his chest.

And that's when he saw her.

Not Lisa.

Ellie.

The face below him changed, morphing in his mind—

Rain on the windshield. The sound of tires skidding. Her voice, young and trembling—*Daddy?*

Eric's breath caught. The memory crashed over him like a wave.

His hands loosened.

Lisa gasped, air rushing into her lungs. She coughed, chest heaving, tears streaming down her face. For a moment, neither of them moved.

Eric stared down at her, seeing his daughter's face superimposed over Lisa's. The same wide eyes. The same terrified expression from that night in the rain.

"Ellie?" he whispered.

Lisa blinked up at him, confused, desperate. She tried to speak but could only manage a hoarse whisper. "Please..."

The word broke the spell.

Reality crashed back. This wasn't Ellie. This was Lisa. It was happening again.

His hands moved without his permission, muscle memory and panic taking over.

Lisa's eyes widened as his grip tightened again.

She tried to say his name, but no sound came.

Her hands clawed weakly at his wrists. Her body convulsed once—twice—

Then went still.

Eric blinked.

Lisa lay beneath him, her face slack, eyes staring at nothing.

What have I done?

The thought hit him like ice water. This wasn't some faceless threat. This was Lisa. Sweet, innocent Lisa who used to stay after class to talk about books. Who laughed at his stupid jokes. Who once told him he was the only adult she could trust.

Who was seventeen years old.

His hands were still around her throat. He jerked them back as if burned, stumbling to his feet.

"No, no, no..." The words came out as a whisper, then louder. "Lisa? Lisa, wake up."

But she didn't move. Couldn't move.

He'd killed her.

The garage spun around him. His chest tightened, breath coming in short gasps. This couldn't be happening. Not again. He was supposed to be fixing things, protecting what was left of his family, making sure no one else got hurt.

Instead, he'd destroyed everything.

Again.

Buster whimpered from the corner, trying to stand on shaky legs.

Eric didn't look at him.

He just stared at Lisa's body.

As if waiting for her to wake up.

As if willing time to reverse itself.

As if seventeen years hadn't just ended because of his hands.

CHAPTER 33

*O*ne Year Ago

It was raining.

Not hard, just steady enough that the wipers had to stay on low. A rhythm like a heartbeat across the windshield.

Eric kept glancing at the clock on the dash. 7:42am. They were late. Again.

Ellie sat in the passenger seat, flipping through a stack of index cards, her lips moving silently.

"Test today?" he asked, forcing his voice to sound casual.

She nodded without looking up. "Geometry."

He grunted in sympathy. "You'll do fine. Like always."

No response. She was already lost in the flash cards again.

The light ahead turned red. He eased the car to a stop.

The interior smelled like wet jackets and the vanilla lip gloss Ellie always wore.

She hummed under her breath, some pop song he didn't recognize. She'd been quieter lately.

Laura said it was normal. Teenagers pulled away. Especially girls.

But that hadn't made it easier.

The light turned green. Eric tapped the gas.

"Hey," he said, glancing over. "You want Taco Bell after school? Your mom's working late."

Ellie looked up at last and smiled. It was small, but it was real.

"Yeah," she said. "Can I get two burritos?"

"Two?"

"I'm growing, daddy. You gotta accept it," she said, rolling her eyes.

Eric laughed. "Deal."

And that was the last thing either of them said.

Because the car in front of them stopped.

And Eric didn't.

He saw the brake lights a second too late.

He slammed the pedal.

Tires screamed.

Metal folded in on itself.

Ellie's scream.

Glass.

Then silence.

He came to with blood in his mouth.

The windshield spiderwebbed. Airbags hung deflated.

Ellie wasn't moving.

"Ellie?" he choked. "Ellie!"

Sirens wailed somewhere nearby.

Time fractured.

An ambulance. A stretcher.

Laura at the hospital, her voice cracked with rage—*You killed her. You killed our baby.*

No one said it was his fault. Not officially.

But it didn't matter.

Laura kicked him out three months later.

No screaming. No tears.

Just a note on the counter. A box by the door.

His old college hoodie. A shaving kit.

The photo of the three of them at the pumpkin patch.

He didn't take the photo.

He didn't take much of anything.

He didn't argue. What was there to say?

She was right to hate him.

He just left.

Moved across town. Took a new job. New school. New name on the door.

Rented a studio that smelled like mildew and smoke.

The silence followed him.

He didn't decorate or hang anything on the walls. He just unpacked what he needed—sheets, dishes, clothes.

The rest stayed in boxes.

Stacked in the closet like headstones.

The only sounds in the apartment came from the fridge when it kicked on, or the cars passing on the freeway outside.

But most nights, it was just him.

And the memories.

The last look Ellie gave him before everything shattered.

The sound of her humming in the passenger seat.

The smell of her shampoo in the car.

He lived with those things like they were still alive.

Because in his mind—

Sometimes they were.

He told himself Ellie was just away at college, busy with classes.

Exactly where she would have been. He said it so often that he started to believe it.

He didn't keep a shrine. He didn't speak to her out loud.

But he left space for her.

In the quiet.

In the way he still bought two burritos for her.

In the way he avoided the road where it happened.

She wasn't dead.

She was just... not home.

And on nights like this, when the silence screamed too loud—

That lie was all he had left.

CHAPTER 34

The hallway stretched longer than it should have.

Every shadow looked wrong. Every sound felt like a whisper he couldn't quite catch.

"Lisa," Tyler called, voice hoarse. "Lisa, I'm coming. Please hang on."

He passed the kitchen. The living room. Then the door to the garage. Shut tight.

Buster's leash lay tangled in the entryway, the end frayed.

He heard a noise behind the door.

A thud.

Then silence.

He threw himself at it.

"Lisa!"

It groaned under his weight, but didn't open.

He ran to the laundry room, remembering the narrow door that connected to the garage, just behind the dryer.

His hand trembled as he turned the knob.

It creaked open.

The flashlight beam wavered as he stepped inside.

And stopped.

Lisa lay on the cold concrete floor.

Her eyes were open, but empty.

She wasn't moving.

Beside her, Buster stood frozen, ears flat, tail low. He didn't bark.

He didn't need to.

Tyler dropped the flashlight and the poker, collapsing to his knees. "No—no, no, no—"

He touched her cheek. It was still warm.

The smell of bleach mixed with blood. The quiet hum of the freezer. Tyler forced himself to look, even as his vision blurred. He wanted her to move, to breathe. But she didn't.

"Lisa," he whispered. "Please..."

He shook her slightly.

But she didn't blink.

Didn't breathe.

Tyler's hands curled into fists.

And then—

From the shadows at the edge of the garage, something shifted.

A step.

The scrape of a boot.

He looked up.

Eric stood there.

Quiet.

Watching.

His face unreadable.

And Tyler, who had no weapon, no plan, no time, stood to face him anyway.

CHAPTER 35

Katie ran barefoot through the wet grass, the keys digging into her palm.

Her breath came in short, ragged gasps. Evelyn's body was still in the corner of her vision, even though she wasn't looking anymore.

Don't think about that.

Just get to the car.

She slid into the driver's seat of Tyler's Camaro and slammed the door shut.

Locked it.

Her fingers shook as she jammed the key into the ignition, turned it once. Nothing.

Her stomach dropped. She'd forgotten the clutch.

"Come on," she whispered, her voice breaking, as she pressed her foot down and tried again.

This time, the engine sputtered, then caught, roaring to life.

She grabbed the car phone and dialed.

9-1-1.

Her fingers slipped on the buttons.

Ring.

Another ring.

"9-1-1, what's your emergency?"

"There's someone in the house," she said, her voice shaking. "He killed our neighbor and...and my friends are still in there. He's going to kill them too. You have to hurry."

"Okay, ma'am, I need you to stay calm. What is your location?"

Katie gave the address in a rush.

"Officers are on their way. Are you in a safe location?"

She turned to look at the house.

Dark windows stared back at her like blind eyes. One door hung wide open, spilling blackness onto the porch.

"No," she whispered. "I don't think I am."

CHAPTER 36

Eric didn't speak.

He stood in shadow, breathing slowly. Watching.

Tyler's eyes adjusted just enough to catch the lines of his face.

Recognition hit like ice in his veins.

"Wait," he whispered. "Mr. Donner?"

Eric didn't respond.

Tyler blinked, heart pounding. "What's going on?"

Still no answer. Just a slow, deliberate step forward.

"I don't understand—"

Lisa's body was still behind him—cold, still, crumpled like a broken doll.

Tyler's jaw trembled. "*You* killed her?"

Eric's face didn't change.

"You killed Lisa," Tyler said, louder now. "You fucking killed her."

Something flickered in Eric's eyes. Maybe regret. Maybe not.

Then, he moved.

Fast.

Tyler barely got his arms up before Eric barreled into him.

The force slammed him into the wall, sending tools crashing to the floor.

Eric's hands found his throat—tight, unrelenting.

Tyler choked, feet scrambling, fists punching wild and wide.

A direct hit to the jaw. Nothing.

Another to the ribs. No reaction.

Eric's grip tightened.

The edges of the world began to fade.

Then—

A snarl.

Buster.

The little dog launched from the dark with everything he had.

His teeth sank into Eric's forearm.

Eric cried out, staggering back, trying to shake him off.

Tyler fell, gasping, coughing on the floor.

Buster held on. Growling. Pulling. Refusing to let go.

It was enough.

Tyler dragged himself upright, grabbing the fire poker with shaking hands. His ribs screamed, every breath like fire, but he kept moving. He had to.

But Eric didn't come for him again.

He looked past him.

At Lisa.

And something cracked.

Eric's face went slack. His eyes blurred.

Then came the sirens, loud and closing fast.

Red and blue light slashed across the garage.

Eric turned, blinked into the color like he didn't understand it—

And ran.

Out the side door.

Tyler dropped the fire poker and fell to his knees.

Blood dripped from Buster's mouth as he limped to Tyler's side, pressing against his hip, trembling.

They didn't say anything.

There was nothing left to say.

CHAPTER 37

The sirens came fast. Red and blue strobed across the windshield like fireworks exploding underwater.

Katie's hands gripped the steering wheel, slick with sweat. She didn't even realize the car was still running until the engine sputtered beneath her.

The dispatcher was still on the line, calm but distant.

"They're here," Katie whispered. "Thank you for staying on the phone with me."

Two squad cars screeched to a stop in front of the house.

Doors flung open.

Officers spilled out, hands on their weapons, flashlights already cutting across the lawn.

Katie pressed her forehead to the steering wheel, a sob catching in her throat.

Please be okay. Please be okay.

"Front door's open!" one officer barked. "Approach with caution!"

Katie flinched.

Then—

The door creaked.

Someone stepped out.

Tyler.

Staggering. Covered in blood.

And just behind him—

Buster.

The little dog padded close at his side, body low, ears flat, tail between his legs.

Still alive. Still with him.

The officers raised their weapons immediately.

"Hands in the air!"

Tyler froze.

A flashlight beam pinned him in place.

"Do it now! Hands where I can see them!"

He lifted his arms slowly. "I—I'm not—he's still inside—"

Katie threw the car door open. "Wait! That's my friend! He's not the guy!"

"Stay back, kid!" one of them snapped.

Another officer moved in cautiously, patting Tyler down and dragging his hands behind his back.

"Don't move. What's your name?"

"Tyler," he rasped. "Please. It's not me. He might still be in there."

The officer hesitated, eyes locked on his.

"Who might still be in there?"

Tyler panted, fighting for breath. "Mr. Donner. He's our teacher. He killed our friend. And her neighbor. He bolted when he heard the sirens."

Silence.

Then—

"Clear the house," one of them barked.

Two officers rushed up the porch steps, guns drawn.

Katie darted around the car and dropped to her knees beside Tyler.

Buster pushed in between them, leaning against her legs, shaking.

Tyler looked up. His face crumpled.

"It was Mr. Donner," he said hoarsely.

Katie blinked. "What?"

Her breath caught in her throat. The name didn't register at first.

But then it did.

Mr. Donner.

Their teacher.

The man from the phone call.

Her stomach turned. Memories flooded her: his voice in class, his laugh in the hallway. The way Lisa used to talk about him. The way they'd all thought he was a bit creepy.

"He killed her," Tyler whispered. "He killed Lisa."

Katie shook her head like she hadn't heard him right. Tyler stared at nothing, as if trying to make sense of it himself.

"No," she said. "No... she was just..."

Her voice broke.

There was no just anymore.

She pressed a hand to her mouth, choking back a sob.

Lisa was gone.

And the man who had done it was someone they knew. Someone who had smiled at them in class. In the school hallway. Buster let out a low whine and nudged Katie's hand. She closed her fingers around his fur and didn't let go.

CHAPTER 38

The ambulance screamed away with Tyler inside, its siren dopplering into the distance. Behind Katie, the coroner's van waited with its engine running. Katie kept her eyes fixed ahead, refusing to watch them load what remained of Evelyn and Lisa into the back.

She stood frozen in the driveway, arms wrapped tight around herself. Wind swept through the oak trees, tugging at her sleeves. Everything around her—police radios crackling, neighbors huddled in bathrobes, the urgent shuffle of boots between both houses—dissolved into white noise.

Buster stood tense at her feet, fur prickling, golden eyes locked on Lisa's house.

A growl rumbled deep in his throat. Soft. Guttural. Katie followed his stare.

The porch light flickered its broken morse code. The front door gaped open.

"Full sweep complete on both properties." An officer's voice cut through the static. "He's gone."

Then another voice burst from a radio, clipped and urgent: "We've got a body twenty miles out, off County Road Nine. Badge confirms—it's one of ours."

Heads snapped up. Orders barked. Flashlights swung as officers scrambled for their cruisers, engines roaring, sirens splitting the darkness.

The street emptied in seconds. Only one or two cops lingered.

No one was watching the house anymore—except Katie and Buster.

And in that flickering porch light, something moved behind the door.

Katie's feet were already moving. She told herself she just wanted to grab something from Lisa's room. A hoodie. A necklace. Something normal.

But the truth pressed harder with every step. She needed to see it. She needed proof that Lisa had really been here, had lived here, right up until she didn't.

Her throat tightened.

If she didn't step inside now, she'd never be able to. And then it would be gone—sold, emptied, erased. Just another house on another street where something terrible happened.

Buster's body locked. His growl deepened, low and guttural, vibrating through the boards beneath her.

She didn't look back.

She crossed the threshold. And the door whispered shut behind her.

The living room was a quiet ruin—popcorn on the rug, soda dried to sticky patches, the Cosmo quiz with scribbled answers half-torn on the coffee table.

The stereo still played softly.

She didn't recognize the song, but the lyrics cut like a knife.

...somebody save me / I'm close to the edge...

Her throat closed. She moved down the hallway. Up the stairs.

Past Lisa's mom's room. Past the bathroom.

She stopped at Lisa's door.

It was open a crack.

The light was off.

Katie reached for the switch. Clicked it. Nothing.

The power was still out.

She pushed the door open slowly.

The scent hit her first.

Vanilla lotion. Lip gloss. Old perfume and laundry detergent.

The air was heavy with it. Katie stepped into the room like she was crossing into a shrine.

Lisa's bed was unmade. A sweater hung limply over the desk chair. Her nightstand lamp was unplugged, the cord coiled like a question.

Everything was still.

Too still.

She moved further inside, her breath tight in her throat.

Then she heard it.

A soft creak.

Katie froze.

She glanced up.

The attic door in the ceiling—barely noticeable—was slightly ajar. The string hung down, swaying just slightly, like it had been disturbed.

She stepped back—

And that's when it happened.

A sound behind her. A slow, sliding thud.

She turned—

And he was there.

Standing in front of her.

Still.

Silent.

His eyes met hers in the dark.

Katie's lungs seized. She couldn't move.

Eric turned his head, and smiled.

"You came back," he whispered.

Katie's heart slammed against her ribs.

Her feet were cemented to the floor.

"They searched the whole house," she said. "You weren't here."

"I was hiding in the attic," Eric said. "I didn't know where else to go."

His gaze drifted around the room, his fingers trailing across Lisa's blanket like it was sacred. "She would've loved this room," he murmured.

"Who the fuck are you talking about, you asshole?" Katie screamed.

"Ellie, my daughter. She always loved spaces like this."

In the faint light from the hallway, Katie could see the blood matted in his hair. The way his hands twitched at his sides. She backed slowly toward the desk. Her fingers brushed the heavy ceramic base of Lisa's lamp.

She gripped it. But didn't lift it.

Not yet.

"Lisa's gone because of you," Katie cried.

"I didn't mean for any of this to happen," Eric said.

"You're our teacher," Katie replied, as if realizing it for the first time. "You were supposed to protect us."

Eric's face crumpled, something raw and broken flashing through his eyes.

"I failed all of you," he murmured. "And I failed Ellie."

He took a shaky step forward.

Katie raised the lamp.

"Don't," she warned.

Eric's breath caught. "I didn't see the car," he whispered. His voice frayed like torn cloth. "One second it wasn't there and then she was just...gone."

His eyes glazed, staring past her. "I can still hear it sometimes. The tires. The glass. The way she screamed. And then...nothing. Just silence."

His shoulders sagged, his lips trembling. He wasn't speaking to her anymore. He was speaking to himself, chasing the memory like it might undo itself if he said it enough.

Katie's hands shook. Her chest burned. "What makes you think I give a shit? You killed my friend!"

That broke whatever was left.

Eric lunged.

She swung the lamp.

It cracked across his jaw.

He hit the dresser, knocked it askew.

Katie grabbed the drawer handle and yanked it out, threw it at him.

He ducked and charged again.

She stumbled back, grabbed the nightstand. The alarm clock tumbled. She swung the drawer like a shield.

Eric grabbed her arm.

They struggled and crashed into the bookshelf.

It toppled. Books and trinkets spilled across the carpet.

Katie shoved him off.

Buster's bark tore through the hallway.

Then claws on wood. A flash of fur.

Buster launched himself into the room.

His teeth found Eric's ankle.

Eric screamed in pain.

Katie didn't wait.

She grabbed Lisa's heavy jewelry box and slammed it against Eric's temple.

He went down hard.

Didn't move.

Didn't breathe.

Just lay there, blood pooling into the rug.

Buster backed off slowly, still growling.

Katie stumbled back, panting. The jewelry box slipped from her fingers and hit the floor with a dull clatter. Her hands shook, her legs almost giving out. Her stomach lurched.

She took one shaky step backward.

Then—

Eric's hand snapped up and grabbed her ankle.

Katie screamed, collapsing hard onto her side. Her elbow slammed into the floor. The breath whooshed from her lungs.

Eric pulled, dragging her back toward him, one hand now on her calf, the other clawing for the lamp.

"I wish she never called me tonight," Eric whispered.

Katie froze. "It...it was just a coincidence," she stammered.

"No," he said. "She said she knew. She said she missed me."

"Missed you?" Katie's stomach turned. Her chest tightened.

And then the realization hit.

Lisa had known it was Donner on the other end of the line. She had wanted to call him. All the times she had teased her about Mr. Donner, laughed it off like it was nothing...

It hadn't been nothing.

"Please stay with me," Eric hissed, breaking her out of her thoughts.

"No!" she screamed, kicking at him with everything she had. Her bare foot struck his cheekbone. He didn't let go.

She grabbed the edge of Lisa's dresser, fingers scrambling for something—anything.

Her hand closed on a glass perfume bottle.

Katie swung.

It shattered against Eric's temple with a wet crunch. Sweet perfume sprayed everywhere. Lisa's scent mixing with blood.

Eric recoiled. This time, he let go.

Katie rolled away, dragging herself to her feet. She turned to him and really looked at him.

He wasn't Mr. Donner anymore.

Just a ruin of the man they'd known. Something broken. Something hollow.

"Ellie," he whispered to her.

"I'm not Ellie," Katie said, breath ragged. "And you don't get to take me too."

Katie stared at his crumpled body, her chest rising and falling in sharp, uneven bursts. Blood pooled beneath him, darkening the carpet Lisa had once picked out herself.

She waited. For him to move, to open his eyes, to lunge again. Her own heartbeat thundered so loud she almost couldn't hear the silence pressing down around her. But nothing came.

The room was wreckage. The overturned lamp, the shattered picture frame, the stuffed bear in the corner missing an eye. Lisa's world reduced to rubble.

And all she could think about was Lisa's mom.

Coming home to this.

To a daughter she thought was safe.

To a house that should've protected her.

Katie's chest clenched. The thought made her stomach twist in a way the blood never had.

Only when Buster nudged her—his warm head burrowing into her lap—did she breathe again. She sank to the floor, clutching him as though he were the only real thing left in the world. Tears slipped down her cheeks, silent and salty, disappearing into his fur.

The silence held. Long enough for her pulse to slow. Long enough for her to think maybe it was finally over.

Then—

Footsteps. Pounding down the hall.

A voice shouted—"Clear!"—and then:

An officer stepped into the doorway, gun drawn.

He froze when he saw them.

Katie.

Buster.

And Mr. Donner's body on the floor.

"Jesus," the officer breathed. "Are you hurt?"

Katie opened her mouth, but no words came.

She just looked at him, then at Mr. Donner, unmoving in the middle of Lisa's rug.

"I got him," she said finally. "I think I got him."

The officer holstered his weapon and knelt beside her. "You sure did," he said. "It's over now."

She leaned her face into Buster's fur and for the first time all night, she let herself believe it.

She was safe.

CHAPTER 39

The sky was just beginning to lighten, soft streaks of pink and gray bleeding into the edge of dawn.

Katie sat on the front steps of the Turner house, a wool blanket wrapped around her shoulders, her eyes swollen and raw.

She wasn't cold.

She wasn't anything.

The police had finished with their second set of questions. The ambulance had taken Mr. Donner's body away in silence, like even the sirens were too loud now.

Lisa was gone. And Katie didn't know how to live in a world without her.

Tyler was alive, they said. Banged up, bruised, but stable.

That word—stable—sounded strange in a world where nothing felt steady anymore.

Katie stared at the grass, at the patches of overturned dirt where boots had trampled flower beds.

The blanket smelled like smoke and antiseptic.

Beside her, Buster sat curled against her thigh, his body warm, his breathing steady.

Someone had tried to take him earlier—an officer asking if she knew where the dog belonged.

Katie had said, quietly, "He's with me now."

No one questioned it.

Buster hadn't left her side since.

His fur was sticky with blood near the collar, but he didn't whimper.

He was a survivor, just like her.

She reached down and stroked behind his ears. His tail thumped once, slow and steady.

The sun began to rise.

She was glad it was Saturday. She needed sleep. Needed to process everything.

Buster shifted beside her, leaning his head against her leg, his breath warm against her skin.

An officer approached, speaking softly into a radio.

"Did you reach your parents?" she asked.

"No, I didn't want to worry them."

"I can drive you home."

"Thanks," Katie said.

She stared straight ahead, eyes burning.

She didn't know what came next.

But she wasn't alone.

EPILOGUE

The first day back at Ridgewood High was quiet in a way schools never should be. No laughter in the halls. No music echoing from locker speakers. Just the hollow echo of sneakers on tile and the occasional whispers.

The story had been on the news all week. Every channel, every update seemed to say the same thing: *Ridgewood High teacher kills student and four others.* Pictures of Lisa. Of Mr. Donner. Of his wife. Her lover. Evelyn. And a police offer. Police tape. Flashing lights outside Lisa's house. The anchors said her name over and over until Katie had to keep the TV and radio off just to keep from screaming.

Outside, news vans still clustered near the front gates, their satellite dishes turned skyward. A few reporters stood with microphones ready, hoping for a tearful quote or a glimpse of someone who knew Lisa before they moved on to the next big story. The principal kept giving statements about counseling services and safety measures, but nobody really listened.

It had taken Katie a full week to come back. Even then, she wasn't sure it was the right decision.

She kept thinking about Lisa's mom standing at the graveside, completely still, her face unreadable under the gray sky. She hadn't cried, not while anyone was watching. She'd just stared at the casket like she was waiting for someone to tell her it was all a mistake. That Lisa was fine. That this wasn't real.

Katie had wanted to say something. Anything. But what could you possibly say to a mother burying her daughter?

That moment stuck with her more than anything else. Not the blood. Not the screams. Just that look—the absence of hope.

She walked the halls now like a ghost. People stared but didn't speak. A few teachers offered tight, uncomfortable smiles. One even placed a hand on her shoulder and whispered, "Glad you're back," like it meant something.

She appreciated the silence more.

In her backpack was a folded piece of paper. The school counselor had printed out grief resources and written "If you ever want to talk" at the bottom in looping cursive.

Katie hadn't unfolded it.

She passed the science wing and paused. The door to Room 216 was shut. A new name already replaced Mr. Donner on the placard beside it.

Katie turned and kept walking.

Lisa's locker was still there. Unopened.

A small memorial had formed. A flower taped to the vent. A Post-it note shaped like a heart. A tube of pink nail polish, capped and untouched.

Lisa hadn't deserved to become a story people whispered about.

She deserved to be here.

Katie adjusted the strap of her backpack and turned toward the stairs.

That's when she saw him.

Tyler.

He was standing at the far end of the hall, just outside the attendance office. His arm was still in a sling, and he looked thinner, like someone who hadn't eaten right in a while. But he was there. And he was watching her.

For a moment neither of them moved.

Then he started toward her. Slowly at first, then faster.

Katie's breath caught as he closed the distance.

When he reached her, he didn't say anything. He just pulled her into him, his good arm wrapping tight around her shoulders. She clung back, burying her face against his chest.

No words. No explanations. Just the relief of two people still alive.

When they finally let go, Katie stepped back, wiping at her eyes.

"I'll call you later," she whispered.

He nodded, voice rough. "Bye, Katie."

Katie turned toward the stairs as Tyler walked the other way. Near the vending machines, Ben sat on the edge of the bench, hunched over a notebook, headphones on but not playing anything. His Crestfield Pizza windbreaker was balled up beside him. He was scribbling something, head down, as if staying still might make everything feel less fractured.

Katie wondered if he missed her too. If he still looked at the empty chair beside him in Chemistry class.

She didn't stop. But she saw him.

And somehow, she knew he saw her too.

After school, when Katie stepped outside, the midday sun was bright and unseasonably warm. The kind of day that made the world look normal, even when it wasn't.

She paused on the top step, squinting against the sunlight. Her chest ached in that deep, invisible way it had ever since that night, but she was still breathing. Still here.

She let the warmth settle on her face for a second, trying to take comfort in it. Then something made her look across the street.

A man stood by the fence near the trees. Watching the school. Watching her.

Her heart skipped.

Mr. Donner.

He was just standing there. Still. His face unreadable, eyes locked on hers.

A school bus rolled by, blocking her view for a few seconds with the screech of brakes and the low murmur of students inside.

When she blinked, there was nothing but empty pavement and shadows. Of course there was. He was dead. She had to keep reminding herself of that.

But still, she stayed there for another minute, heart pounding, eyes wide, wondering if she'd see him again.

She didn't.

Eventually, she adjusted the strap on her backpack and stepped off the curb. Her footsteps found their rhythm, but they felt strange, like they belonged to someone else. Someone older. Someone changed.

Each step carried her further from that night— and further from the girl she would never be again.

UPCOMING THRILLERS BY SEBASTIAN GREGORY

Phantom of the Galleria

Evil Stepmother

ABOUT THE AUTHOR

Sebastian Gregory grew up in Los Angeles, California, where he fell under the spell of 1990s horror and never escaped its grip. Today, he channels that lifelong obsession into writing teen-focused, nostalgia-driven thrillers reminiscent of the books that once kept him turning pages until dawn. When not writing, Sebastian can be found devouring books, watching movies, or plotting his next travel adventure. He lives in Las Vegas, Nevada, with his family and pets, and teaches creative writing full-time. *We Know Your Secret* is his debut novel.

www.ingramcontent.com/pod-product-compliance
Lightning Source LLC
Chambersburg PA
CBHW020802310726
48969CB00002B/654